# WOLVES OF CHERNOBYL

*Wolves of Chernobyl*



This is a work of fiction. Names, characters, places, and incidents are products of the author's imagination or have been used fictitiously and are not to be construed as real. Any resemblance to persons, living or dead, actual events, locales, or organizations is coincidental.

ISBN: 979-8-9893424-8-8 (hardback)
979-8-9893424-7-1 (paperback)

Printed in the United States of America

# WOLVES
## OF
# CHERNOBYL

GARY J. ROSE

To Gillian McDonald,

Your guidance, keen eye, and unwavering dedication have transformed mere words into a symphony of meaning. With every stroke of your editorial pen, you have sculpted this narrative into its truest form, illuminating its depths and refining its essence.

Thank you for your unparalleled expertise, your tireless commitment, and your boundless passion for the craft. This novel bears witness to your brilliance and stands as a testament to the invaluable contributions of an exceptional editor.

# PROLOGUE

On February 11, 2024, while much of the world tuned into their television sets in anticipation of the Super Bowl showdown between the Kansas City Chiefs and the San Francisco 49ers, headlines across various news outlets unveiled a startling discovery.

Within the desolate confines of Chernobyl's former disaster zone, where the specter of a nuclear meltdown still loomed, reports emerged of mutant wolves roaming the deserted streets exhibiting an unprecedented resilience to cancer.

*Wolves of Chernobyl* evokes a sense of mystery and intrigue surrounding the aftermath of the nuclear catastrophe. It suggests the events unfolding in the story are not just isolated incidents but reverberations of a larger, more ominous presence lurking within the contaminated landscape.

With its haunting imagery and thematic resonance, *Wolves of Chernobyl* promises to captivate readers, drawing them into the eerie and terrifying silence of a world humanity had hoped to forget.

# CHAPTER ONE

## NIGHTFALL

The night of April 26, 1986, descended upon the sleepy town of Pripyat with an eerie stillness masking the impending catastrophe that loomed on the horizon. The streets, usually bustling with activity, were shrouded in a disquieting silence as residents settled into their homes, unaware of the imminent danger that awaited them.

The Zhukov family gathered for a quiet evening together in a modest apartment nestled within the heart of Pripyat. Dmitri, a dedicated factory worker with a rugged exterior but a gentle heart, sat at the dinner table with his wife, Anya, a kind-hearted schoolteacher known for her unwavering compassion.

Their children, young Sasha and his older sister, Natalia, spun tales of their day at school safe within their modest yet snug apartment in the shadow of what would soon become the Chernobyl exclusion zone. Their laughter weaved a tapestry of warmth and joy in the otherwise quiet space, and the anticipation of the upcoming May Day celebration infused the air with excitement as they eagerly planned their adventures.

Natalia's eyes sparkled with mischief as she declared her intention to conquer the towering heights of the Ferris wheel, her youthful bravado on full display. "I'll soar high above the world," Natalia proclaimed proudly, her confidence shining through as she accepted her brother's challenge. She teased Sasha, suggesting he was afraid of heights, a notion he vehemently denied with a playful grin.

"Not afraid, just cautious," Sasha countered, his competitive spirit rising. "Besides, I'd rather be in a bumper car, ready to give you a friendly bump!" he teased, his words dripping with mischievous intent as he envisioned the playful collisions they would share.

Their parents watched with fond amusement as the playful banter between their children unfolded before them. Their smiles mirrored the joy radiating from their offspring, a testament to the bond shared by this close-knit family. Amid uncertainty and hardship, moments like these served as precious reminders of the resilience of the human spirit and the enduring power of love and laughter.

"Well, if we are going to get up early, beat the May Day parade crowd, and be the first in line for the amusement park rides, we'd better help momma clear the table and get ready for bed." Sasha and Natalia quickly jumped to attention and began clearing the kitchen table while continuing to boast about who was the bravest.

Dmitri woke from a restless sleep and noticed his alarm clock showing 1:23:58 a.m. A loud explosion echoed throughout Pripyat's apartment complexes as Dmitri processed the time. He leaped out of bed and ran to the window.

A worried Anya called out to him in the darkness, "What is it?"

Dmitri's worst nightmare had become reality. Flames could be seen coming from the Chernobyl nuclear reactor. "It's the reactor. There has been an explosion. We must get the kids and get out of here quickly."

Alarmed whispers echoed through the streets, mingling with the distant wail of sirens. Dmitri exchanged a worried glance with Anya, a knot of fear tightening in his chest as he realized something was dreadfully wrong.

Hurriedly, they ushered their children into the cramped confines of their car, joining the frantic exodus of panicked residents fleeing the encroaching disaster. With each passing moment, the air grew thicker with the acrid scent of smoke, and an ominous glow illuminated the night sky, casting sinister shadows upon the deserted streets.

Desperate to escape, Dmitri navigated Pripyat's labyrinthine roads with a sense of extreme urgency, his hands trembling on the steering wheel as he prayed for the safety of his beloved family. However, as they neared the outskirts of town, a sudden barrage of chaos erupted around them, trapping them in a nightmarish maelstrom of fear and confusion.

With no time to spare, Dmitri made a split-second decision, veering off the main road in a desperate bid to find an alternate route to safety. However, fate had other plans, and disaster struck with devastating force before they could reach their destination.

The ground trembled beneath them as a deafening roar filled the air, signaling the catastrophic explosion of the Chernobyl Nuclear Power Plant. In the blink of an eye, their world was engulfed in a blinding flash of light followed by a wave of searing heat that consumed everything in its path.

In the ensuing chaos, Dmitri's grip on the steering wheel faltered, and their car careened off the road, crashing into a ditch with bone-jarring force. Time seemed to stand still for a moment as the smoke and debris settled around them, casting a pall of despair over the shattered remnants of their once-cherished dreams.

As Dmitri struggled to regain his bearings, he turned to his family with a mixture of anguish and determination, his heart heavy with the knowledge that their chances of survival were rapidly dwindling. With tears streaming down his cheeks, he gathered them close, whispering words of love and reassurance in the face of the unspeakable tragedy.

However, as they braced themselves for the inevitable, a sense of quiet acceptance washed over them, binding them in a final, fleeting moment of unity. And as the darkness closed in around them, they took solace in the knowledge that, though their journey had come to an abrupt and untimely end, their love would endure, echoing through the corridors of time like a beacon of hope amid despair.

As the Zhukov family found themselves stranded amid the chaos of the Chernobyl disaster, the world around them had transformed into a nightmarish tableau of destruction and despair.

Pripyat's once-familiar landscape had been warped beyond recognition, its streets littered with debris and wreckage as far as the eye could see. Buildings lay in ruins, their skeletal frames silhouetted against the sickly glow emanating from the stricken reactor in a haunting reminder of the catastrophic chain of events that had unfolded with terrifying speed.

The air was thick with the acrid stench of smoke, while ash mingled with the metallic tang of radiation that hung heavy in the atmosphere. The ground beneath their feet trembled with each aftershock in a grim testament to the raw power unleashed by the explosion.

Amid the devastation, the once-vibrant town was reduced to a ghostly shadow of its former self. Once teeming with life, the streets now lay eerily deserted save for the occasional flicker of movement as survivors stumbled through the wreckage in search of refuge.

Panic rippled through the populous in a wave, fueling the frantic exodus of terrified residents desperate to escape the encroaching danger. Mothers clutched their children close, their faces etched with fear and disbelief as they fled into the unknown while the specter of impending doom haunted their eyes.

However, amid the chaos and despair, a strange and unsettling beauty lingered in the air in the form of a faint but unmistakable glow that suffused the landscape with an otherworldly radiance. It was a stark reminder of the unseen forces at work, invisible tendrils of radiation that seeped into every crevice, leaving their marks on the land for generations to come.

And as the Zhukov family huddled together amid the wreckage, their hearts heavy with sorrow and uncertainty, they knew their journey was far from over. For in the wake of the Chernobyl disaster, they would embark on a new chapter of their lives, one fraught with danger and despair yet infused with a flicker of hope that refused to be extinguished.

By daybreak, Dmitri learned that he and his family had been lucky. The official death toll that night directly attributed to Chernobyl, as recognized by the international community, was thirty-one people, with the UN later saying it could be at least fifty. But amid the grim reality of the situation, a glimmer of relief washed over him as he realized that his family had survived the disaster's initial onslaught.

Still, their future remained uncertain, and the specter of radiation loomed ominously over their heads, casting a long shadow across their hopes and dreams. With each passing moment, the true extent of the tragedy became painfully clear, and Dmitri knew that they would need all the strength and resilience they could muster to navigate the treacherous road ahead.

# CHAPTER TWO

## FALLOUT

Decades have passed since the nightmarish events of April 26, 1986, yet the scars of the Chernobyl disaster still mar the landscape, casting a pall of fear and uncertainty over the once-thriving region.

As the dust settled and the initial shock began to fade, the Soviet authorities scrambled to contain the fallout from the catastrophe, desperately trying to conceal the true extent of the radiation release and its devastating impact on human health and the environment.

In a bid to downplay the situation's severity, the government embarked on a campaign of misinformation and denial, dismissing reports of elevated radiation levels and downplaying the public health risks. Meanwhile, behind closed doors, scientists and officials grappled with the daunting task of mitigating the disaster's long-term consequences, from contaminated soil and water sources to the lingering threat of radiation-induced illnesses.

An evacuation order was issued for Pripyat and surrounding areas amid the chaos and confusion, forcing thousands of families to abandon their homes and livelihoods in desperate bids to escape the invisible threat lurking in their midst.

Convoys of buses and trucks rumbled through the deserted streets in the dead of night, ferrying terrified evacuees to safety as the ominous glow of the stricken reactor loomed on the horizon in a constant reminder of the dangers that lay in wait.

But after the human inhabitants fled the contaminated zone, a silent and haunting landscape remained, where the echoes of their former lives lingered like ghosts in the wind. Abandoned buildings stood as silent monuments to a bygone era, their crumbling facades bearing witness to the passage of time and the ravages of neglect.

And amid the desolation, a strange and surreal sight greeted those brave enough to venture into the forbidden zone: the once-tended fields and forests had been reclaimed by nature and transformed into a twisted wilderness teeming with life. Wild animals roamed freely, their numbers swelling in the absence of humans, while domesticated livestock wandered aimlessly through the abandoned streets, their plaintive cries echoing through the silent ruins.

As the years stretched on, the exclusion zone became a living testament to the resilience of nature and the enduring legacy of human folly, a stark reminder of the fragility of life in the face of unchecked hubris and the destructive power of nuclear technology. And among the desolation and decay, the Chernobyl disaster remained etched in humanity's collective memory as a cautionary tale of the dangers of playing God with forces beyond our control.

A chilling phenomenon emerged from the desolation and decay of the Chernobyl exclusion zone that captured the attention of scientists and researchers worldwide. Studies conducted within the irradiated wilderness uncovered evidence of mutated wildlife, including the enigmatic presence of mutant wolves.

These creatures, once ordinary inhabitants of the region, now bore the unmistakable signs of genetic aberration, their forms twisted and distorted by the radiation's relentless onslaught. Deformed limbs, abnormal growths, and altered behavior patterns were among the visible manifestations of their mutations, serving as haunting reminders of the catastrophic nuclear meltdown that had forever altered the landscape.

Yet, these mutant wolves had carved out a precarious existence within the devastated exclusion zone, adapting to their toxic surroundings with an eerie resilience. Freed from the constraints of human civilization, they roamed the desolate wilderness, their howls echoing through the silent ruins as they hunted among the shadows.

But while Chernobyl's mutant wolves had become emblematic of the disaster's enduring legacy, their presence also raised troubling questions about the long-term effects of radiation exposure on both wildlife and human health. As scientists grappled with the implications of their findings, a sense of urgency pervaded their research efforts, driven by the need to unravel the mysteries of Chernobyl's silent inhabitants before it was too late.

Yet, even as their investigations yielded new insights into the nature of mutation and adaptation in the face of adversity, the mutant wolves remained enigmatic symbols of the inherent dangers of nuclear technology. Their presence served as a sobering reminder of the fragile balance between humanity and the natural world and the profound impact of our actions on the world around us.

# CHAPTER THREE

The sixteen-month-old doe threaded cautiously through the forest, heading toward the tranquil stream nestled within Containment Zone #1. Oblivious to the demarcation between zones 1 and 2, her sole focus was on quenching her thirst and staying close to her mother and fellow does.

As the young animal lowered her head to sip from the stream's clear waters, she remained unaware of the silent predator lurking in the nearby shadows. Suddenly, a mutant wolf, its fur mottled with patches of strange colorings, emerged from the underbrush with a swift and deadly grace. Its movements were stealthy, and its approach was silent as it closed the distance between itself and the unsuspecting doe.

In a flash of primal instinct, the wolf pounced, its razor-sharp teeth sinking into the doe's vulnerable neck. A moment of startled panic flickered in the doe's eyes before being extinguished by the predator's merciless grip. With a chilling finality, the wolf's attack was swift and lethal, leaving the young doe lifeless beside the tranquil stream; her peaceful quest for water was abruptly ended by the mutant predator's savage force.

As the gory scene unfolded, a more sinister presence lurked in the shadows, observing the brutal attack with a hunger that surpassed even that of the mutant wolf. This creature, a grotesque amalgamation of twisted features and malevolent intent, waited patiently for the wolf to begin consuming its prey. With a guttural growl that reverberated through the forest, it launched forward with astonishing speed, eclipsing even the swiftness of the mutant wolf's attack.

The monstrous entity overpowered the wolf in a flurry of claws and fangs, its relentless assault ending the predator's life in a violent blur. With both the doe and the wolf now lying lifeless at its feet, the abomination reveled in its gruesome triumph, savoring the prospect of not one but two succulent meals. As the forest fell silent once more, the chilling presence of this monstrous predator served as a grim reminder of the dangers lurking within the depths of Containment Zone #1.

As the monstrous creature stood over its fallen victims, a chilling realization dawned: it was not merely an animal but a twisted semblance of humanity, walking upright on two legs with an eerie glint of intelligence gleaming in its eyes. With a guttural grunt of satisfaction, it seized the limp bodies of the doe and the mutant wolf, its unnaturally strong arms effortlessly dragging the lifeless forms deeper into the heart of Containment Zone #1.

The forest whispered with dread as the creature disappeared into the shadows, its grotesque silhouette blending seamlessly with the darkness, leaving an unsettling aura of menace and mystery in its wake.

"Who's winning?" Willie Cole chimed in, entering the front room with a bag of chips and a bowl of warmed nacho cheese sauce in hand. Tall, with a Michael Jordan bald head and broad shoulders, Willie had once been a star wideout for the University of Notre Dame until a devastating ACL injury had shattered his dreams of making it to the NFL. Settling into a seat near the television, he eagerly tuned in to watch the San Francisco 49ers kickoff to the Kansas City Chiefs. It was February 11, and the 58th Super Bowl was taking place in Allegiant Stadium in Paradise, Nevada, next to Sin City, Las Vegas.

"Who cares?" Tan Eng responded, his attention momentarily diverted from a scientific journal he was reading. Slightly perturbed by Willie's question, Tan shifted his gaze from the pages before him. "Just a bunch of overpaid jocks, pampered most of their lives, smashing into each other. I can't believe that a sane individual would plop down $7,000 to $77,000 to buy a ticket."

Tan stood as a beacon of intellectual prowess within the group, a distinction considering the caliber of minds assembled. His brilliance was not merely a matter of opinion; it was a fact acknowledged by all who knew him.

Tan's academic journey had begun with a meteoric rise, culminating in a Ph.D. from Yale University at the tender age of seventeen. Yet, he didn't just have one Ph.D. but two in the fields of cellular biology and mathematics, a testament to his exceptional aptitude across multiple disciplines.

The world seemed to lay itself at Tan's feet following his graduation. Silicon Valley giants and clandestine government agencies alike vied for his attention, each recognizing the extraordinary potential harbored within this young prodigy. The CIA extended their hand, seeking to enlist his formidable intellect for matters of national security, while top tech firms eagerly courted him, hoping to harness his genius for the next wave of technological innovation.

However, Tan's path diverged from the conventional trajectories that lay before him. Instead of succumbing to the allure of power and prestige offered by Silicon Valley or the intelligence community, he chose a different calling rooted in a deeply personal and profound sense of purpose. Tan pledged his allegiance to Heath and his team, driven by an unwavering resolve to confront a formidable adversary: cancer.

The disease had already exacted a heavy toll on Tan, claiming the lives of both his parents. These searing losses fueled his determination to devote his unparalleled intellect and skills to the pursuit of a cure. Tan found kindred spirits in Heath and his team, as they were united by a shared mission and a collective resolve to confront the scourge of cancer head-on.

As Tan stood among his peers, his decision to forgo the allures of wealth and power in favor of a nobler cause spoke volumes about the depth of his character and the magnitude of his conviction. In a world where brilliance was often synonymous with ambition and self-interest, Tan's choice stood as a testament to the transformative power of empathy and the enduring legacy of love.

"Hey, just because football isn't a thing in China, Tan, doesn't mean you have to diss my boys," Willie retorted with a grin, his loyalty to the 49ers unwavering. "You're witnessing history in the making right here, with the 49ers clinching their sixth championship. Come on, let's crank up the volume and savor the moment!"

Heath Sterling, the group's leader, sat at a dining room table alongside Christina Lauren, his girlfriend of the past two years. Though the Super Bowl played in the background, their attention was fixed on a detailed map of the Chernobyl evacuation zones, meticulously studying the locations of guard posts.

Heath, like Tan, had received training in cellular biology at Yale and held a Ph.D. Christina, once Heath's student intern, had since become an integral part of their team and their relationship had blossomed into an intimate partnership.

In the gathering, among the esteemed company of Heath and Christina, stood Monica Bennett and Jack Crawford, both wielding formidable oncology medical degrees. While their relationship wasn't defined by romantic entanglements like that of Heath and Christina, there existed between them a bond forged in shared passion and mutual respect, often seeking solace in each other's presence amidst the challenges of their profession.

Monica's brilliance shone brightly, having graduated at the zenith of her class from Harvard Medical School. Despite possessing the intellect and skill to excel as a medical practitioner or specialist, she, much like Jack, recognized the profound potential for impact in the realm of medical research, particularly in the field of oncology. With her slender frame, short reddish hair, face peppered with freckles, and a countenance that belied her true age, Monica exuded an air of youthful determination and tenacity.

On the other hand, Jack cut a figure of understated strength and resilience. Towering above most with his tall stature and sporting an average build, he possessed an unassuming charisma that drew people to him effortlessly. His long brown hair, tied back in a casual ponytail, framed a face adorned with a beard and mustache that seemed to perpetually linger in a state of unkempt charm, a testament to his perpetual focus on matters far beyond the trivialities of personal appearance.

Despite their outward differences, Monica and Jack shared a common vision and dedication to advancing the frontiers of oncological research, recognizing the potential to alleviate suffering and save lives on a scale far greater than what could be achieved through individual clinical practice. And as they stood among their peers, their presence spoke volumes of their unwavering commitment to the noble cause they had chosen to champion.

Willie Cole and Stu Cornfield, undergraduates who had joined Heath's team out of a lack of other prospects, completed the group. Willie, known for his strength, handled the heavy lifting of equipment, while Stu, affectionately dubbed 'Cornflake,' was responsible for electrical hookups.

As the game progressed into the fourth quarter and the Chiefs were on the verge of tying, everyone in the group, except Tan, became fully engrossed in the intense matchup. The table in front of them was now laden with chili, garlic bread, pizza, wings, and sweet and sour meatballs, along with more chips, salsa, and cheese sauce. Empty beer cans littered the floor, evidence of the excitement and tension that filled the room.

As the game entered overtime, Heath couldn't help but feel a twinge of disappointment, knowing that he had wanted to go over tomorrow's plan one last time before everyone retired for the night. Despite his concerns, the group remained fixated on the game, with Heath trying to conceal his frustration as the clock ticked down.

With just thirteen seconds left on the clock, the Chiefs scored a game-winning touchdown, much to the dismay of Willie, who continued to criticize the 49ers' head coach for his play calling.

"Alright, sorry about your loss, Willie," Heath said, mustering a smile as he addressed his disappointed friend. "But let's gather around the dining room table for one last check of our procedures early tomorrow morning. Stu, is the van filled with gasoline?"

"To the top," Stu replied confidently. "Couldn't squeeze in anymore if we tried. I've also checked the air pressure in our tires, including the spare. Non-perishable food is already stowed in the back. Tomorrow, first thing, I'll load the rest of the food and supplies inside."

"Good. And did you ensure all our technical equipment is securely strapped down, including the supply of tranquilizer darts? Two guns?"

"Check and check," Stu replied.

"Jack and Monica have already mixed what we will be using, ketamine in combo with alpha-2 sedative and diazepam. That is an overdose, so once we take a few wolves down, we won't have to add too much sedation," Heath added.

"How long will they be out? I don't want to be withdrawing their blood when they come out of their sleep," Tan asked.

"The dart should knock them out in one to five minutes, and hopefully, they won't get too far after that. Once down, they should be out for between fifteen and thirty minutes," Monica replied.

Heath paused and established eye contact with everyone present in turn. "Listen up. We've all read the latest news accounts about the mutant animals inside Pripyat, specifically the wolves. That's why we are here. I know some of you are here for the money and fame of capturing mutant wolves inside the Chernobyl containment area. Some, more for the money, while Tan here wants the fame of potentially finding a cure for cancer. Right, Tan?" Tan nodded. Everyone laughed.

"Frankly, your motivations don't interest me. I'm more concerned about getting in and out without being discovered and avoiding any injuries. I don't know if the guards are trigger-happy, but it appears their rounds of the containment zones are sporadic at best. More significantly, I have no idea what would happen to us if we were caught.

"That said, please look at the map one last time. We'll cut the outer fence wire here," he pointed to the perimeter. "Afterward, we'll retreat into the forest and wait to see if the fence triggers an alarm that prompts the guards to respond. Assuming it's clear, we'll follow this route, Willie, slow and steady, with no lights on, please," indicating a road. "The roads, as can be expected, are in poor shape as Mother Nature continues to reclaim her domain.

"Our destination is this apartment building in the center of Pripyat. Once inside, Monica, you and Christina will black out the windows before we start up our generator, which Willie will bring in. Stu, you'll hook it up first thing so we can survey our surroundings inside the building.

"Assuming everything goes as planned, we will set up the equipment, make our bedding, and get something to eat."

Suddenly, Christina excused herself from the meeting and dashed down the hallway to the bathroom. "Guess someone can't hold her beer," Willie quipped with a smirk. The group could hear Christina vomiting from the bathroom area.

"Could have been the nachos," Stu chimed in, a mischievous grin spreading across his face as he and Willie shared a laugh.

"Leave her alone, you two," Monica interjected, her tone tinged with concern. "She's been battling an upset stomach for the past few days. If it were you two babies, she and I would have to nurse you back to the living."

"Are you two through?" Heath's stern gaze fell upon Willie and Stu, who lowered their heads without responding. "After we secure our location, Jack and I will scout the area before dawn to see if we can locate any signs of wolf packs. We'll then set up traps accordingly.

"Remember, there are two containment zones. The outer zone is approximately 30 km wide, while the inner zone is 10 km. It is safe to stay in the outer containmnet zone overnight, but we only have a brief time inside the inner zone.

"The wolves we will attempt to catch were exposed to upwards of 11.28 millirem of radiation every day for their entire lives, which is more than six times the legal safety limit for a human. This has apparently altered their immune systems in a similar way to cancer patients undergoing radiation treatment, but more significantly, specific parts of the animals' genetic information seem resilient to increased cancer risk." Heath turned to Tan, who took over.

"The mutant wolves that roam the human-free Chernobyl containment zone have developed cancer-resilient genomes that could be key to helping humans fight the deadly disease. These wild animals somehow have managed to adapt and survive the high levels of radiation. Capturing a few of these wolves and then drawing and testing their blood might reveal how their body organisms adapted, and then, with additional testing, we can create a cure for cancer. That is my motivation."

"Tan, I understand your eagerness to set up equipment, but we need to establish the guards' routine first. So, while Jack and I are out, you and Stu will start noting their patrol patterns. Is that clear to everyone?"

A resounding chorus of yesses filled the room, save for Monica, who had just rejoined the group. "Alright, people, we have a big day ahead of us tomorrow, so let's get some sleep," Heath concluded, ushering the group toward their respective sleeping quarters.

Heath lay on his back, looking at the ceiling. There was enough light from the moon, so as the rain hit the bedroom window, a random pattern appeared above him. Christina walked in, removed all her clothing, and climbed on top of Heath.

"Are you worried about tomorrow?" she asked as she noticed her nakedness had aroused Heath.

"Yes. We are not trained Navy SEALs. It is not just avoiding detection but confronting these wolves in a contamination zone. There are so many variables to consider."

She reached for his manhood. "Maybe I can help take your mind off these things so you can get a good night's sleep."

# CHAPTER FOUR

Christina and Heath were the first to stir from their slumber. "I'll rouse the others. Maybe you can start brewing some coffee," Heath suggested as he hastily dressed. Glancing at his watch, he noted the early hour: 3 a.m. "If any of them give you trouble about waking up, just give me a heads-up, and I'll handle it," Christina said, adding a wink. Heath decided to wait and watch Christina pull on her pants and shirt over her underwear.

Remarkably, by 3:40, everyone had managed to grab a quick bite to eat, sip their coffee or tea, and get dressed, assembling in the black Mercedes Sprinter van. Due to his size, Willie occupied the front passenger seat, with Heath taking the driver's position. The others settled in among the equipment stored in the back, making themselves as comfortable as possible for the journey ahead.

"We'll be reaching the outer fence of Containment Zone #2 in about an hour and a half, so if anyone wants to catch a nap, now's the time," Heath announced to the group at large. "Christina, could you pour me a cup of coffee?" he added, directing his request to her. Christina promptly grabbed a thermos and filled a Styrofoam cup with coffee, handing it over to Heath while purposefully rubbing one of her breasts against his shoulder. He blew her a playful kiss before taking a sip.

"I've gotta admit, Heath, this whole Chernobyl thing – it scares the living daylights outta me," Willie confided in a low voice, making sure his words stayed between them and didn't carry to those seated further back in the van. Meanwhile, Monica and Jack were engrossed in examining some photos of the area post-disaster.

"I saw pictures of a Ferris wheel, bumper cars, and a deserted swimming pool in that book Monica and Jack are reading. Gave me goosebumps, I swear," he added, his voice tinged with a mix of unease and fascination. He rubbed his bald head with his left hand.

"Relax," Heath reassured, trying to keep their conversation private. "It's just a bunch of abandoned buildings. Concrete and whatnot. No dead bodies strewn about. Everyone made it out except for those unfortunate souls near the blast zone. Look at it this way: Imagine you're married, living with your wife and kids. Suddenly, an alarm blares, like a tornado warning. You've only got a few minutes to grab the most essential items before you have to flee, leaving most of your belongings behind."

Willie pondered deeply, digesting Heath's words. "Now, let's imagine, after the tornado or whatever disaster passes, you and your family return. If you're lucky, your house and everything in it are still intact. Your kids' toys, your sports magazines, all just where you left them. But with Chernobyl, you have to factor in the radiation. You can't go back. It's an evacuation. The things you left behind are gone forever.

"That's what we're likely to encounter when we step into these abandoned housing units. Personal belongings, lost, never to be seen or touched again." Willie remained silent for the rest of the trip.

"Alright, folks, we've arrived," Heath announced, rousing Willie from his slumber along with several other team members who had dozed off. "There's still plenty of moonlight, so we'll hold off on using flashlights. We don't want to attract any passing security details. Can someone grab the wire cutters?" He glanced at Willie. "Willie, would you do us the honor of cutting away the fencing so we can drive the van through?"

Within half an hour, Willie had removed a sizable portion of the fencing. Heath maneuvered the van through the gap and then waited patiently as Willie and Stu meticulously reattached the fencing using thin lengths of wire, ensuring their actions wouldn't draw any unwanted attention.

With Willie and Stu settled back into the van, they set off toward the cluster of housing units where they aimed to stay while also hoping to encounter a few mutant wolves. Heath drove cautiously, refraining from using the van's headlights.

"Does anyone have any insight into why the wolves didn't react to the significant radiation levels before and why they seem unaffected now?" Stu inquired.

"I believe, Stu, that the best individuals to address that question are our esteemed oncologists, Jack and Monica," Heath replied, looking up into the rearview mirror to see Monica and Jack.

Monica glanced at Jack, a silent communication passing between them before she turned her attention back to Stu's question. "It's a complex issue," she began, her tone measured. "Radiation affects different organisms in various ways. In some cases, exposure can lead to immediate illness or death. However, in others, like these mutant wolves, it's possible they've developed some form of resilience or adaptation to the radiation over time."

Jack nodded in agreement. "Exactly. It's a phenomenon known as radiation hormesis. In certain organisms, low levels of radiation exposure can actually stimulate biological repair mechanisms and enhance resilience to subsequent exposures. Over generations, this could lead to the development of organisms that are more tolerant to radiation."

Stu furrowed his brow, absorbing the information. "So, you're saying these mutant wolves might have evolved to tolerate the radiation here in Chernobyl?"

Monica nodded, "It's certainly a possibility. Nature has a way of adapting to extreme environments, and Chernobyl, despite its dangers, has become a unique ecosystem where some species have managed to thrive despite the radiation."

Jack chimed in, "And don't forget, the absence of human interference could also play a role. With fewer humans around, there's less hunting pressure and habitat destruction, allowing these mutant wolves to establish themselves more successfully in the area."

Stu nodded, his curiosity piqued. "Fascinating. It's incredible how resilient and adaptable nature can be, even in the face of such extreme challenges." As the van rumbled on through the darkened landscape of Chernobyl, the team continued to discuss the intricacies of the ecosystem they were venturing into, each member marveling at the resilience of life in the shadow of disaster.

Abruptly, Heath slammed on the brakes, bashing the team members in the rear of the van into each other. "What the hell!" exclaimed Tan, clearly annoyed as he nursed a bump on his head.

"Quiet, everyone! Look," Heath commanded, pointing toward two vans parked outside the housing unit he had selected for them. "Damn it. Someone's here." They all strained through the darkness to see if they could see any movement. Nothing stirred.

"What do we do now?" Christina inquired.

"Let's sit tight for a few minutes and see if anyone comes or goes from either van," Heath suggested. Just then, a large wolf, unseen until now, darted from the front of one of the vans into the abandoned housing units.

"Did you see that? That wolf was huge," Tan exclaimed with excitement.

"Shh!" Heath hushed them. "No one speak. Roll down your window, Willie." Willie complied, and the group fell into silence for several minutes.

"What are we listening for?" Monica finally asked, hoping to understand Heath's plan.

"It's not what we're hearing, it's what we aren't hearing that surprises me," Heath replied. "How could a mutant wolf enter what we believe to be our competitors' housing quarters without anyone screaming or firing gunshots? Nothing."

A heavy silence settled over the van in response to Heath's question. Each member of the team found themselves grappling with their thoughts, formulating answers they were hesitant to voice aloud. Uncertainty hung in the air, mingling with a sense of apprehension as they contemplated the implications of the situation before them.

Christina shifted uncomfortably in her seat, her mind racing with possibilities but unwilling to voice her fears. Willie's brow furrowed as he pondered the potential dangers lurking outside, his silence a testament to the weight of his concerns. Tan's eyes darted nervously from face to face, unable to shake the unease that gripped him, yet hesitant to admit his anxieties.

Monica and Jack exchanged a meaningful glance, and silent communication passed between them as they mulled over the situation. Despite their expertise, even they found themselves at a loss for an explanation, and the unsettling silence of the abandoned housing units left them with more questions than answers. Christina had moved forward and her right arm was resting on Heath's shoulder for reassurance.

Amid the collective unease, Heath's voice broke through the tension, his tone reflective yet determined. "We need to proceed with caution," he declared, breaking the oppressive silence that had enveloped them. "Stay alert and keep your eyes peeled. We can't afford to underestimate the dangers of this place."

"I'll park the van over there, near the other housing unit. Willie, Tan, you two stay here with the ladies," Heath directed.

"Not a problem," a relieved Willie affirmed.

"Stu, Jack, and I will sneak up from the side," Heath continued, his tone resolute. "Stu, grab one of the tranquilizer guns and load a dart. We don't have any handguns, so that will have to do. Alright, let's move." With a shared nod of agreement, the trio exited the van, their determination palpable as they prepared to face whatever challenges awaited them.

As the night enveloped the abandoned housing complex in an eerie silence, Heath, Stu, and Jack moved stealthily through the shadows, their senses alert for any sign of movement. The air hung heavy with tension as they advanced cautiously, their footsteps muffled against the debris-strewn floor.

Heath was the first to enter one of the rooms, and the grinding sounds of bones being broken and something being devoured echoed ominously through the desolate corridors. With a silent gesture, he motioned for Stu and Jack to follow him, their hearts pounding in their chests as they braced themselves for what they might encounter.

Rounding a corner, their worst fears were realized in a scene of unimaginable horror. Several partially consumed bodies lay strewn across the floor, blood pooling around them in macabre puddles. At the center of it all, the wolf they had glimpsed earlier tore into its grisly meal with frenzied abandon, oblivious to their presence.

With steady hands, Heath raised the tranquilizer gun, taking careful aim at the ravenous predator. In a swift motion, he fired a dart into the wolf's flank, eliciting a howl of pain and surprise. Startled, the beast bolted past them, its movements fueled by fear and adrenaline.

As the sedative swiftly took effect, the formidable wolf succumbed to its tranquilizing embrace, its once-proud form now crumpled mere yards away from where they stood. Approaching cautiously, a somber gravity settled over Heath and his companions, the magnitude of the crisis they faced becoming all too real as they drew nearer to the scene of carnage.

"Man, look at its fur. Something seems off, doesn't it?" Heath's voice broke the heavy silence as he and Jack edged closer to the sedated wolf, their gazes fixated on its mangy coat. Tentatively, Heath reached out to touch the downed creature, his fingers brushing against its coarse, matted fur.

"It's not just matted; it's unlike anything I've felt before," Heath remarked, his brow furrowing in concern. "The texture… it's not soft like a dog's fur. It's almost… wiry and incredibly long. I'm hesitant to stroke against the grain for fear that it might cut like a blade."

Jack and Stu, drawn by curiosity and a sense of grim fascination, joined their companions by the fallen beast, their hands gingerly exploring its fur. "You're right," Stu murmured, his expression one of mild disgust. "It's… gross."

"And check out those fangs," Jack interjected, his voice tinged with a mix of awe and concern as he knelt beside the sedated wolf. "They seem a lot longer than any wolves I've seen, even in zoos. Looks like the radiation really did a number on him."

Heath and the others leaned in, their eyes narrowing as they took in the sight of the wolf's elongated canines gleaming in the faint moonlight filtering through the window. The once-majestic features of the creature now bore the unmistakable scars of its exposure to Chernobyl's toxic legacy, a poignant reminder of the devastating impact of mankind's hubris.

"It's not just the fur," Heath murmured, his gaze lingering on the wolf's formidable jaws. "The whole morphology seems… distorted. Radiation-induced mutations, obviously."

The implications of their discovery weighed heavily upon them, casting a pall over the room. In the wake of the Chernobyl disaster, nature had been twisted and contorted in ways that defied comprehension, giving rise to a new breed of predators forged in the crucible of nuclear catastrophe.

As they pondered the significance of their findings, the distant howl of another wolf echoed through the night as a haunting reminder of the dangers that lurked within the shadowy depths of the exclusion zone.

They stood in the presence of the sedated wolf as the peculiarity of its fur served as a grim reminder of the profound mysteries they were about to unravel. With each passing moment, the urgency of their mission grew, driving home the reality of the perilous journey that lay ahead ever deeper into the heart of darkness in search of answers and, perhaps, redemption.

# CHAPTER FIVE

"Alright, we can't risk the girls seeing any of this," Heath whispered urgently. "Let's haul this wolf outside and see if Monica can draw some blood quickly. Then, we'll regroup in the van and get out of here."

"What about that?" Jack asked, pointing back to the room with the remains.

"Nothing can be done for them. They will eventually be found, and we can use that commotion to conceal our research for the short time we will be here.

Stu and Jack nodded, each grabbing hold of a hind leg and heaving the massive wolf out of the blood-soaked scene and into the outer hallway. Heath gestured for the rest of the team in the van to join them. As they gathered around the wolf, Heath briefed them on what he, Stu, and Jack had witnessed in the interior room. Then, turning to Monica, he instructed her to prepare her equipment and draw blood from the wolf before it regained consciousness.

With the task completed, they hurried back to the safety of the van, locking the doors behind them as they retreated from the eerie scene, their minds racing with the implications of what they had just encountered.

"Alright, spill it," Willie demanded, his voice tense with disbelief. "How many bodies did you find? And how on earth did a wolf manage to get in there and attack them without anyone noticing? And why the hell didn't we hear anything?"

Tension rippled through the van, sparking a flurry of nervous chatter. "Quiet down!" Heath's voice sliced through the noise, instantly silencing everyone. "Willie, all valid questions, but panicking won't do us any good. Let's approach this logically."

Locking eyes with each member of the group, Heath continued, "First off, let's assume those folks were here for the same reason we are. I counted seven bodies. Stu, Jack, does that match what you saw?"

"Yeah, that sounds about right," Jack confirmed while Stu nodded in agreement.

"Now, consider this," Heath began, his tone measured as he addressed the group. "I find it highly improbable for a single wolf, even if it's mutated, to take down seven adults and create the level of carnage we witnessed."

Tan furrowed his brow, his expression mirroring the confusion shared by Christina and the rest of the team. "So, if it wasn't the wolf, how did they meet their demise?" he queried, anticipation evident in his voice as he awaited Heath's explanation. The others leaned in, eager for insight into the unfolding mystery.

As the group huddled in the confines of the van, Heath's mind raced with unsettling possibilities. "What if," he pondered, "the victims weren't killed by the lone wolf we encountered but rather by a pack of wolves?" The thought sent a shiver down his spine. It seemed more plausible that the devastation they had witnessed was the result of a coordinated attack by multiple predators.

"But then," Heath mused aloud, drawing the team's attention, "what if the wolf we stumbled upon was merely a scavenger? What if it had come across the aftermath of the attack and seized the opportunity to feed?"

The notion made sense and cast a pall of unease over the group. If that were the case, it meant there could be more wolves out there, lurking in the shadows, waiting for their next opportunity to strike. It was a grim realization, one that only deepened the sense of foreboding pervading the abandoned town of Chernobyl.

Heath's gaze swept over his companions, noting the mixture of apprehension and determination etched on their faces. They were in uncharted territory, facing a threat unlike anything they thought they would encounter. But despite the fear that gnawed at their insides, they knew they couldn't turn back now. They had come too far, and the truth they sought lay just beyond the veil of darkness that enveloped Chernobyl.

"Okay, let's entertain the idea that it was a pack of wolves," Jack proposed, gesturing toward the sedated beast visible through the window. "What's our next move? We've got just one sample from this wolf, and we're powerless to help those unfortunate souls back there."

"I believe our best course of action is to keep moving forward. We need to find another housing project far removed from here and maintain the façade that we're still on schedule," Heath replied.

"Check this out!" Monica exclaimed, peering out the side window of the van. Still groggy and unsteady, the wolf attempted to wander away from the housing complex. As the team debated their next steps from the relative safety of the van, unbeknownst to them, several two-legged mutant monsters skulked in the shadows, silently observing their every move from a distance.

Heath ignited the van's engine, the rumble echoing through the desolate streets. This time, he flicked on the headlights, casting a feeble beam into the darkness that enveloped Chernobyl. With a determined set to his jaw, he executed a swift U-turn, steering the vehicle away from the abandoned housing development and onto a litter-strewn city street.

The van rattled over potholes and debris as it rolled onward, each bump and jolt serving as a grim reminder of their perilous journey. If only Heath had spared a glance into his rearview mirror, he would have borne witness to the tragic fate of the wolf whose blood they had harvested.

Behind them, bathed in the wan glow of the van's taillights, the wolf's final moments played out in a macabre tableau. Surrounded by the two-legged mutant monsters, the once-majestic creature met a grisly demise, torn apart by ravenous jaws and clawed hands.

But Heath kept his eyes fixed on the road ahead, his focus unwavering as he guided the van deeper into the heart of darkness that was Chernobyl. The distant howls of unseen creatures echoed through the night, a haunting reminder of the dangers that lurked just beyond the headlights' reach.

And as they pressed on, each mile brought them closer to the unknown horrors that awaited. Heath couldn't shake the feeling that they were being watched, hunted, by something far more sinister than wolves. It was as if the very shadows themselves harbored malevolent intent, a darkness that hungered for their souls.

"This housing unit seems suitable," Heath remarked, his gaze sweeping over the abandoned block of apartments. "It's far enough from the previous spot and offers a bit more seclusion. Considering we've already obtained one sample and today has been draining, I suggest we focus on getting our gear inside, preparing a decent meal, and unwinding."

Heath paused, casting a glance at Monica and Christina. "With nighttime descending early and no power available, we'll need to fire up the generator. To avoid sounding presumptuous, I suggest Monica and Christina take charge of getting food started while the guys bring in the gear."

Silence greeted Heath's directives, but the team wasted no time in carrying out their assigned tasks. "Let's position the generator over there," Heath instructed, pointing to a corner near a window for ventilation. "And we'll set up our medical equipment against that wall. Overhead lights should go there, too, since that's where we'll be working the most."

As Willie entered, bearing two dart guns and a suitcase filled with drug compounds and extra darts, he inquired, "Where do you want these?"

"Pass them over," Heath replied, taking the dart guns from Willie. "We'll fortify that door and use that broken table, or whatever it was, to cover the window. I'll bunk down by the window with one of the guns, just in case. Willie, you take the other gun and face the door."

With a sense of urgency, the team sprang into action, transforming the abandoned apartment into a makeshift base of operations. They worked swiftly, driven by the knowledge that the dangers lurking outside were far from imaginary. Within an hour, food was ready, and the equipment was stored.

# CHAPTER SIX

With their appetite satisfied, the group gathered in a circle facing a smaller gas lamp that hummed as it burned. "I wonder what it was really like on the night of the explosion and meltdown?" Christina asked no one in particular.

Tan surprised everyone by volunteering to answer her question. "Pripyat was a town that once thrived in the shadow of towering mountains, its beauty a testament to the resilience of the human spirit. But on that fateful day, when the earth shook and the sky turned ashen, Pripyat was forever changed.

"Picture it. A crisp morning, the air tinged with the promise of spring. The townsfolk went about their daily routines, unaware of the catastrophe that loomed on the horizon. Children laughed and played in the streets while merchants peddled their wares in the bustling market square. Life in Pripyat was simple yet vibrant, a testament to the bonds of community that held the town together.

"But then, without warning, the ground trembled beneath their feet, and a deafening roar echoed through the valley. Panic swept through the streets like wildfire as buildings crumbled and streets buckled under the force of the explosion. In an instant, the tranquil town of Pripyat was transformed into a scene of chaos and devastation.

"Amid the chaos, families were torn apart, their cries drowned out by the roar of the inferno consuming everything in its path. The once-idyllic streets were now littered with debris and rubble, the air thick with smoke and ash. Those who were fortunate enough to survive fled for their lives, their homes reduced to smoldering ruins.

"However, amidst the destruction, tales of heroism emerged. Brave souls risked their lives to rescue their neighbors from the wreckage, their selflessness beacons of hope in the darkest of times. In the face of tragedy, the people of Pripyat banded together, united by a common determination to rebuild and recover.

"And so, as the sun set on Pripyat's smoldering ruins, a new chapter began. Though the scars of the disaster would forever mark the landscape, the spirit of resilience endured. And though the town may have been changed, its heart remained unbroken, a testament to the indomitable strength of the human spirit."

"Tan, no offense, but I'm the type who needs all the details," Christina said. "Did alarms blare, or was it a sudden explosion?"

"And what's the deal with the Ferris Wheel and bumper cars?" Willie interjected. "Was there some sort of carnival happening at the time? And how many people were killed on the spot? Like I said to Heath earlier, this situation gives me the creeps."

Jack got up, walked over to his backpack, and pulled out a book. "Maybe this will fill in the gaps. When Heath hit Monica and me up about coming here, I found this book on Amazon and bought it. The beginning of the book gives a chronological list of events." He opened the cover of the novel and began to read the highlights.

"The unit 4 reactor was to be shut down for routine maintenance on April 25, 1986. It was decided to take advantage of this shutdown to determine whether, in the event of a loss of station power, the slowing turbine could provide enough electrical power to operate the main core cooling water circulating pumps until the diesel emergency power supply became operative. The aim of this test was to determine whether cooling of the core could continue to be ensured in the event of a loss of power."

"So, this whole catastrophe occurred due to a test?" Christina asked

"Yes," Jack answered before continuing. "This type of test had been run the previous year, but the power delivered from the running down turbine fell off too rapidly, so it was decided to repeat the test using the new voltage regulators that had been developed. Unfortunately, this test, which was considered essentially concerning the non-nuclear part of the power plant, was carried out without a proper exchange of information and coordination between the team in charge of the test and the personnel in charge of the safety of the nuclear reactor. Therefore, inadequate safety precautions were included in the test program, and the operating personnel were not alerted to the nuclear safety implications of the electrical test and its potential danger.

"As the shutdown proceeded, the reactor was operating at about half power when the electrical load dispatcher refused to allow further shutdown, as the power was needed for the grid. In accordance with the planned test program, about an hour later, the ECCS was switched off while the reactor continued to operate at half power. It was not until about 23:00 on April 25 that the grid controller agreed to a further reduction in power."

"What about what was going on outside the reactors?" Willie pressed, his impatience evident. "The Ferris wheel, the bumper cars, and so on?"

Jack shifted uncomfortably in his seat, the weight of his prior research pressing down on him. "There was, indeed, a carnival set up," he began slowly, his voice tinged with the somber realization of what had transpired. "Pripyat was gearing up for its annual May Day celebrations. The Ferris wheel stood tall against the horizon, its colorful lights promising joy and laughter. The bumper cars awaited eager riders, their neon hues casting playful shadows on the pavement."

Christina's eyes widened as she pieced together the significance of Jack's words. "So, there were people there… innocent bystanders caught in the chaos?" she murmured, her voice trembling slightly.

Jack nodded solemnly. "Yes, there were families strolling through the carnival grounds, children laughing as they anticipated the rides. But then… then, everything changed. The explosion ripped through the air, shattering the tranquility of the evening. Panic ensued as screams drowned out the cheerful melodies of the carnival."

Willie's expression darkened as he absorbed the gravity of the situation. "How many… how many were affected?" he asked, his voice barely above a whisper.

Jack's gaze drifted back to the book, where he found the answer to Willie's question. "The carnage was immense," he replied, his voice heavy with sorrow. "Many lost their lives instantly, their joyful anticipation turned into unimaginable horror in the blink of an eye. Others suffered agonizing injuries, their lives forever altered by the ravages of radiation."

Jack continued reading the timeline of the events. "At 01:23, the power excursion rate emergency protection system signals came on, and the power exceeded 530 MWt and continued to rise. Fuel elements ruptured, leading to increased steam generation, which in turn further increased power owing to the large positive void coefficient. Damage to even just three or four fuel assemblies would have been enough to destroy the reactor.

"The rupture of several fuel channels increased the pressure in the reactor to the extent that the 1000 t reactor support plate became detached, consequently jamming the control rods, which were only halfway down by that time. As the channel pipes began to rupture, mass steam generation occurred because of the depressurization of the reactor cooling circuit. At 01:24, severe shocks occurred as the RCPS rods stopped moving before they reached the lower limit stop switches.

"Two explosions were reported, the first being the initial steam explosion, followed two or three seconds later by a second explosion, possibly from the build-up of hydrogen due to zirconium-steam reactions.

"Fuel, moderator, and structural materials were ejected, starting a number of fires, and the destroyed core was exposed to the atmosphere. One worker, whose body was never recovered, was killed in the explosions, and a second worker died in hospital a few hours later because of injuries received in the explosions.

"Some media reported a seismic origin of the accident; however, the scientific credibility of the paper at the origin of this rumor has been discarded."

Silence descended upon the room. At that moment, they were all acutely aware of life's fragility and fate's mercilessness. Once a symbol of innocence and joy, the carnival grounds had become a haunting reminder of the devastation wrought by human error and hubris. As they contemplated the horrors that had unfolded in Pripyat, they couldn't help but feel a chill creeping into their hearts, knowing some nightmares were all too real.

"Willie," Heath interjected, breaking the heavy silence that enveloped the room. "I just wanted to give you a heads-up. Tomorrow, we'll be in the vicinity of the Ferris wheel, trying to trap a few more wolves. I don't want you to freak out."

Willie's acknowledgment was distant, his mind still grappling with the weight of the revelations.

Jack glanced at Heath, seeking approval to proceed. "Should I continue?" he inquired.

Heath nodded encouragingly. "The more background information the group has, the better. Go on."

"To address your initial question, Willie, regarding the death count," Jack began, his tone measured.

"The true toll of the Chernobyl disaster is difficult to ascertain due to the enduring health repercussions of radioactive contamination. Officially, the international community recognizes just thirty-one fatalities directly attributed to Chernobyl, though the UN suggests it could be as high as fifty."

A heavy stillness descended upon the room, each member processing the gravity of Jack's words. After a moment, Jack pressed on, "However, it's crucial to acknowledge that hundreds of first responders were deployed to extinguish the flames at the nuclear facility and undertake the daunting task of cleaning up the Chernobyl site in the aftermath.

"The estimated number of individuals affected could reach as high as 830,000, yet only 600,000 were granted official recognition, entitling them to significant social benefits such as healthcare and retirement provisions. It's important to remember the affected region was part of the former Soviet Union at the time."

The weight of Jack's revelations lingered, each member of the group grappling with the magnitude of the human tragedy and the complex aftermath of the Chernobyl disaster.

# CHAPTER SEVEN

"I hate to dwell on a morbid topic, pardon the pun, but what became of the animals in the area?" Christina inquired.

Jack swiftly flipped through his book, scanning for the pertinent information. "Most domestic pets perished as radiation permeated the region," he explained. "First responders and emergency personnel euthanized animals they believed could spread harmful radioactive particles. However, some animals, like the wolves, managed to survive.

"Some dogs sought refuge in the first responders' camps, scavenging for scraps of food, and later took shelter in abandoned buildings, like this one, finding solace in the empty spaces. Remarkably, in the 1,600-square-mile exclusion zone around the power plant, they encountered each other and began to reproduce.

"Expanding on that, Christina," Jack elaborated, adjusting his glasses as he delved into the grim details, "Domesticated animals like cows, pigs, sheep, and horses faced culling due to their proximity to human settlements. Their potential to transfer radioactive contaminants into the food chain posed significant risks, prompting authorities to take swift action.

"Furthermore," he continued, "various wildlife species met the same fate in efforts to mitigate their impact on both human health and ecosystem recovery. This encompassed a wide range of creatures, from large mammals like wolves, deer, boars, and elk to smaller animals such as rodents and birds. The rationale behind such measures was to prevent these animals from spreading radioactive materials further and exacerbating the contamination."

Jack paused, the weight of the information settling heavily in the room. "Tragically," he added with a somber tone, "even pets were not exempt from these measures. Some were euthanized to prevent them from wandering out of the contaminated zones, potentially carrying radioactive substances to other regions and further compounding the environmental and health hazards."

The room fell into a heavy silence with Jack's words, each member of the group quietly processing the seriousness of the information. The weight of the tragedies that had unfolded in the aftermath of the Chernobyl disaster was sickening, casting a somber shadow over the discussion.

Christina's brow furrowed as she absorbed the extent of the devastation wreaked upon human and animal populations. The thought of innocent creatures suffering because of human error filled her with a profound sense of sorrow.

Willie's gaze remained fixed on the floor, his mind racing with thoughts of the horrors that had unfolded in the contaminated zone. The sheer scale of the disaster was difficult to comprehend, leaving him feeling a mix of anger and helplessness.

Heath, ever the pragmatic leader, broke the silence, his voice cutting through the heavy atmosphere. "Alright, team," he said, his tone authoritative yet compassionate. "It's time to focus on the task at hand. We need to identify various locations around the abandoned housing projects to place bait for the wolves tonight."

He glanced around the room, noting the solemn expressions etched on his team members' faces. "I know this is a lot to take in," he continued, his voice softening, "but we have a job to do. Let's use this information to inform our approach and ensure we're prepared for whatever we may encounter."

With a sense of renewed purpose, the team began to discuss their plan of action, each member contributing their insights and expertise. As they hashed out the details, a sense of determination settled over them, driving them forward despite the weight of the past.

Finally, Heath suggested they all get some rest to prepare for the evening ahead. "We'll need all our wits about us," he reminded them, "so let's find our bait locations and then take this opportunity to recharge and gather our strength for what lies ahead."

With nods of agreement, the team dispersed, each member retreating to their respective quarters to rest and steel themselves for the challenges that awaited them in the desolate landscape of the abandoned housing projects.

As Ivan and Yuri, two Ukrainian security guards, drove together toward the containment zones, their conversation flowed easily, punctuated by an occasional swig from a shared bottle of vodka.

"Did you hear about the new protocols for checking trespassers?" Ivan asked, his thick accent adding charm to his words.

Yuri chuckled, taking a sip from the bottle before responding, "Da, da, I heard. But who would be crazy enough to sneak into these zones anyway? Only fools would risk it."

Ivan nodded in agreement, his eyes scanning the desolate landscape. "Exactly. Besides, we have better things to do than chase ghosts in the night."

Their banter continued as they cruised through the deserted streets, their headlights cutting through the darkness. As they approached the site where scientists who had received permission to enter the containment zone had set up and visited, they spotted the vans belonging to the now-deceased researchers.

"Look, Ivan," Yuri pointed toward the parked vans. "Those are the scientists' vehicles. They have permission to stay until tomorrow, then they must get their asses out of here. They must be sleeping."

Ivan shrugged nonchalantly, taking another swig of vodka. "Eh, let them sleep. It's not our problem."

With that, they continued their rounds, lazily checking for any signs of trespassers while exchanging jokes and anecdotes. As darkness began to envelop the landscape, they decided it was time to call it a night.

"Enough excitement for one evening," Ivan declared, starting the engine and steering the vehicle toward the containment zones' exit.

Yuri chuckled in agreement, settling back in his seat. "Indeed. Let's leave the ghosts to their slumber." With that, they drove out of the containment zones, the darkness swallowing them as they headed back to their base, leaving behind the mysteries of the abandoned sites for another night.

Two wolves prowled restlessly in the dimly moonlit room, the stale air heavy with the scent of decay. They had not heard the advance of the security truck. Their fur matted with dried blood, they circled each other, low growls rumbling deep in their throats as they vied for dominance. With feral intensity, they snapped at one another, their teeth gleaming in the dim light as they lapped at the remnants of blood staining the floor.

The scene was hauntingly surreal, and the only movement in the desolate space was the wolves tearing into the drying remnants of the scientists' demise. Yet, apart from the grisly feast and the predatory dance of the wolves, no other traces remained of the unfortunate souls who had met their end in this forsaken place.

The silence was oppressive, broken only by the sound of tearing flesh and the occasional snarl of aggression between the predators. The absence of human presence accentuated the eerie atmosphere, leaving the room steeped in a palpable sense of foreboding.

As the wolves continued their macabre meal, their primal instincts driving them onward, the specter of the vanished scientists lingered in the shadows, their fate a grim reminder of the dangers lurking within the abandoned confines of the containment zones.

# CHAPTER EIGHT

The team stood poised and ready for action as Heath glanced at his watch, noting the time: 10:30 p.m. With purposeful strides, he approached a small refrigerator and retrieved several round plastic containers with tightly sealed lids.

"Remember, wolves like to travel in packs. I suggest you let the whole pack enter your site and go after the bait before you shoot one of them. If there is enough time, reload and take out another one. Willie, the swimming pool is in your site, so you can set up in the bleachers as cover."

"Alright," Heath began, distributing the containers among his team members. "Willie, Jack, and Monica take this bait and set it up at site one. Here's your tranquilizer gun, Willie. Once you've immobilized a wolf, Monica will extract its blood. Check your walkie-talkies now."

With practiced efficiency, they confirmed their communication devices were in working order.

Turning to the remaining team members, Heath continued, "Tan, stay here with a radio to guard the fort. Stu, Christina, you're with me." He handed the plastic container containing the bait to Stu. "We'll oversee site two, the abandoned school room. Any questions?" Silence greeted his inquiry.

"Okay then," Heath affirmed, his tone firm. "Once you've collected your sample, notify me and then return here promptly. And please, everyone, exercise utmost caution." With their roles clearly defined and instructions given, the team dispersed to their assigned tasks, each member fully aware of the importance of their mission and the risks that lay ahead.

As the team bid farewell to Tan, they traversed the desolate hallway, their footsteps echoing eerily against the cold concrete walls. Their van loomed ahead as they merged into the main yard, representing a solitary beacon amid the desolation. The air hung heavy with anticipation, a tangible sense of unease settling over the group as they prepared to depart.

Then, without warning, a guttural growl ripped through the silence, reverberating off the decaying walls of the housing complex. The sound shocked everyone; it was primal and menacing, unlike anything they had ever encountered before.

Instinctively, their hearts raced, pulses quickening with a mixture of excitement and fear. Jack's voice quivered with a blend of exhilaration and nervousness as he broke the tense silence. "That doesn't sound like a wolf," he remarked, his words laced with a tremor of uncertainty.

The team exchanged anxious glances; their senses were heightened as they strained to discern the source of the ominous growl. The darkness seemed to press in around them, suffocating and oppressive as if concealing unseen terrors lurking just beyond the shadows.

With bated breath, they stood frozen in place, anticipation coiling in the pit of their stomachs. Every nerve tingled with apprehension; the air was thick with the promise of impending danger.

Then, as suddenly as it had begun, the growl ceased, swallowed by the ominous stillness of the night. Yet, its echo lingered, a haunting reminder of the unknown horrors that lurked within the abandoned confines of the complex.

With trembling hands, they hastened to the safety of their van, the sense of urgency palpable in their movements. As the engine roared to life and the headlights pierced the darkness, they stole one last glance over their shoulders, the memory of that chilling growl etched into their minds.

Little did they know, their journey into the heart of darkness had only just begun, and the true horrors that awaited them would far surpass anything they could have ever imagined.

As Heath and his team arrived at the abandoned school, the atmosphere was thick with anticipation. Surrounding them were scattered remnants of civilization, now reclaimed by nature's relentless advance. Among the debris, the telltale signs of wolf activity littered the landscape, their droppings scattered like ominous breadcrumbs leading the way.

As they took stock of their surroundings, the team's gaze settled on the dilapidated school building, its weathered façade standing as a silent sentinel to the passage of time. It was here that they hoped to execute their plan, utilizing the confines of the classroom they had selected to their advantage.

"This room should do the trick," Heath declared, his voice carrying a note of determination. "It'll provide us with the perfect opportunity to trap the wolf or wolves inside, allowing us to deal with them effectively."

Nods of agreement rippled through the group as they set about preparing their trap. With practiced efficiency, they fortified their position, laying out bait strategically and ensuring every detail was meticulously accounted for.

"Alright, team," Heath announced, his tone brimming with authority. "Let's remember our training and stay focused. We have a job to do, and we need to do it right."

As they awaited the arrival of their elusive quarry, each member was acutely aware of the stakes at hand. The abandoned school, once a bastion of learning, now stood as a battleground in their quest to confront the unknown.

They waited with bated breath, their senses attuned to the slightest sound or movement. In the silence that enveloped them, the echoes of their own heartbeat seemed to reverberate with the weight of their mission.

And as the shadows lengthened and the night descended, they knew that whatever awaited them within the confines of the abandoned school would test their mettle in ways they could scarcely imagine.

The team pivoted on their heels in unison, their attention captured by the haunting melody of wolves' howls echoing through the desolate landscape. The sound, primal and chilling, seemed to reverberate through the very marrow of their bones.

As they listened intently, the rhythmic cadence of the howls indicated a gradual approach, drawing nearer with each passing moment. Tension crackled in the air, mingling with a sense of anticipation as the hunters became the hunted.

"I believe they've caught wind of our bait," Heath exclaimed, his voice tinged with excitement. "Prepare yourselves, everyone. The moment we've been waiting for is upon us."

With hearts pounding and adrenaline coursing through their veins, the team readied themselves for the impending encounter. Heath's hand tightened around the dart gun; his breath held in eager anticipation as he braced for the inevitable confrontation.

In the eerie stillness that followed, the only sound that permeated the air was the collective thrum of their racing hearts, a near-silent testament to the gravity of the moment. As the howls grew louder, drawing nearer with each passing second, the team stood poised on the precipice of the unknown, ready to confront whatever awaited them in the darkness.

The abandoned building, which had an Olympic-sized swimming pool, loomed like a ghostly specter against the backdrop of the night sky, its weathered façade bearing the scars of time and neglect. The remnants of a forgotten past lay within its decaying confines, where echoes of laughter and splashing once filled the air. Now, silence reigned supreme, broken only by the occasional drip of rainwater echoing through the dilapidated halls.

The abandoned swimming pool lay at the heart of the structure, its surface marred by a thick layer of debris and decay. Partially filled with rainwater, the pool resembled a murky abyss, its depths shrouded in mystery and foreboding.

Surrounding it, the crumbling remains of the building bore witness to the passage of time, the dilapidated walls and shattered windows a haunting reminder of the transience of human endeavor. In this desolate landscape, nature had begun to reclaim its dominion, weaving vines through cracked concrete and reclaiming the abandoned space as its own. And amid the wreckage and decay, the abandoned swimming pool stood as a silent sentinel, a testament to the relentless march of time and the fragility of human existence.

"What the hell is that?" Willie exclaimed, his voice tinged with disbelief as he directed the beam of his flashlight toward a mound of excrement nestled near the steps leading into the partially filled abandoned pool.

The light cast eerie shadows across the rotting surroundings, illuminating the mysterious pile with an unsettling glow. Its appearance was unlike anything they had encountered before, a grotesque aberration amidst the desolation of the abandoned complex.

Jack furrowed his brow, his expression contorted with confusion as he examined the strange discovery. "That certainly doesn't resemble the wolf droppings we stumbled upon last night," he remarked, his tone laden with uncertainty.

The implications of their find sent a ripple of unease through the group, each member acutely aware of the potential dangers lurking within the shadows. The abandoned swimming pool, once a place of leisure and recreation, now harbored secrets best left undisturbed.

"Look over here," Monica called, her voice carrying a note of urgency as she pointed to a spot on the ground several feet away from the excrement. "It looks like human footprints."

Willie and Jack hurried over, their footsteps echoing through the abandoned building as they joined Monica at the spot she had indicated. The beam of their flashlights illuminated a set of footprints imprinted on the dust-covered floor, their size and shape sending shivers down their spines.

"Shit, look at the size of those prints," Willie muttered, his voice tinged with disbelief as he crouched down for a closer look. The footprints stretched across the ground, their length and width far surpassing anything they had encountered before.

Jack nodded in agreement; his brow wrinkled in consternation as he examined the prints. "These aren't your average footprints," he remarked, his tone grim. "Whoever made these must have been enormous. They look like some of those doctored-up footprints that 'Bigfoot' hunters tried to sell to the public back then to prove his existence."

An unease settled over the group as they contemplated the implications of their discovery. The presence of such colossal footprints within the abandoned building only served to deepen the mystery surrounding their ghastly environment, heightening the tension that hung thick in the air.

With a sense of trepidation gnawing at their senses, Willie, Jack, and Monica exchanged wary glances, their minds racing with unanswered questions. Little did they know, their investigation into the abandoned building would unearth secrets far darker and more sinister than they could have ever imagined.

"Monica, grab a few shots of those footprints," Jack instructed, his voice tinged with urgency. "We'll need to share them with Heath and the rest of the team when we regroup. And see if you can find something to provide a scale for comparison. Look, there's a tennis shoe over there. Place it next to the print and snap some photos."

Monica nodded in acknowledgment, her fingers deftly retrieving her cellphone as she moved toward the discarded shoe. With careful precision, she positioned it next to the imposing footprint, capturing multiple angles to provide context for its size and scale.

As the phone camera clicked, freezing the moment in time, Willie and Jack looked on with a mixture of anticipation and apprehension. The sight of the oversized footprint juxtaposed with the humble tennis shoe only served to underscore the magnitude of their discovery, leaving them with more questions than answers.

"Good thinking, Jack," Willie remarked, his voice laden with admiration as he watched Monica work. "Let's make sure we document everything we find here. It could be crucial to figuring out what's going on."

Jack nodded in agreement, his gaze lingering on the haunting image captured by Monica's cellphone. At that moment, they were acutely aware of the significance of their discovery and the importance of preserving every detail for further analysis.

"Hey, look, there are some more over here," Jack exclaimed, his voice carrying a sense of urgency as he pointed to a smashed window. "And look here. Is that fur?"

Willie and Monica hurried over to Jack's side, their curiosity piqued by his discovery. Together, they peered through the broken window, their flashlights illuminating the scene beyond. Strewn across the floor were several more sets of oversized footprints.

"Those prints…" Monica began, her voice trailing off as she crouched down for a closer look. "They seem to have indentations of claws, but they're too large to belong to a wolf."

Willie nodded in agreement, concentrating on the footprints. "You're right," he confirmed, his tone grave. "These are unlike anything we've seen before. Whatever made them, it's certainly not your average predator."

Meanwhile, Jack continued to inspect the area around the smashed window, his keen eye drawn to a peculiar sight caught in the jagged edges of the broken glass. "And what's this?" he exclaimed, pointing to a tuft of fur wedged between the shards.

As they gathered around, their flashlights converging on the curious discovery, it became clear that the fur did not correspond to that of a wolf. Its texture was coarse and matted, and its coloration was far darker and more ominous than that of any canine.

Monica pulled a pair of tweezers from her medical kit and removed the fur, placing it in a plastic bag. "I can't wait to analyze this when we get back," she declared.

A sense of unease settled over the group as they contemplated the implications of their findings. Whatever creature had left behind these monstrous footprints and ominous fur remained shrouded in mystery, its presence a haunting reminder of the dangers lurking within the abandoned building.

With their investigation yielding more questions than answers, Willie, Jack, and Monica exchanged wary glances, their minds racing with the possibilities. Little did they know, their encounter with the unknown was far from over, and the true horrors that awaited them would test their courage and resilience in ways they could scarcely imagine.

"Okay. Put out the bait, and we'll take our positions. I hate it here," Willie exclaimed.

# CHAPTER NINE

Inside the dimly lit confines of the abandoned school classroom, Heath, Stu, and Christina waited with bated breath, their senses heightened by the anticipation of the impending encounter. Outside, the unmistakable sound of footfalls echoed through the stillness of the night, drawing nearer with each passing moment. Their hearts pounded in unison in a symphony of apprehension and excitement as they braced themselves for their elusive quarry's arrival.

Suddenly, the silence was shattered by the clamor of snapping jaws and rustling fur as twelve wolves burst into the room, filling the space with primal energy. With cautious determination, the team watched as the wolves approached the bait, their movements calculated and deliberate.

Heath's gaze locked onto one of the largest males, his hands steady as he raised the tranquilizer gun and aimed. With a steady hand and unwavering focus, he pulled the trigger, the dart finding its mark precisely. As the sedative took effect, pandemonium erupted among the pack, and their movements became frenzied and disoriented.

Several wolves turned their attention towards Heath and Christina in the chaos that ensued, their snarls reverberating through the air as they closed in on their prey. With adrenaline coursing through their veins, Heath and Christina stood their ground, their resolve unwavering in the face of danger.

However, before they could react, one wolf lunged forward, sinking its teeth into Heath's forearm with savage ferocity. Pain flared through his body as blood seeped from the wound, staining the floor crimson before the assailant quickly retreated, disappearing into the night with the rest of the pack.

With the adrenaline still coursing through their veins, Heath and Christina exchanged a wary glance, the weight of his injury and the lingering threat of the sedated wolf weighing heavily on their minds. Christina, her expression tense with concern, moved to assess Heath's wound. Her hands were steady as she applied pressure to stem the flow of blood.

"We need to get you patched up," Christina urged, her voice edged with urgency as she guided Heath towards a nearby makeshift first aid kit. With practiced efficiency, she cleaned and dressed the wound, her movements swift and sure despite the chaos that had unfolded around them.

As Heath gritted his teeth against the pain, Stu surveyed their surroundings, his senses on high alert for any sign of further danger. The abandoned classroom, once a sanctuary of learning, now bore witness to the aftermath of their harrowing encounter. Its walls were stained with blood and littered with the scattered remnants of their struggle.

The team knew their task was far from over as they observed the sedated wolf lying motionless on the floor. They needed to regroup and assess their next steps lest they find themselves at the mercy of the unknown horrors lurking within the abandoned building once again.

"We can't stay here," Heath declared, his voice firm with resolve as he surveyed the scene before them. He stood with his freshly wrapped forearm still spattered with blood. "Draw the blood from the wolf. We need to get back to the van and alert the others. Whatever else is out there, we need to be prepared."

Nodding in agreement, the three headed to the classroom door, their determination unwavering despite the exhaustion that threatened to overwhelm them. With one last glance at the sedated wolf, they turned and made their way toward the exit, their minds racing with the myriad challenges lying ahead.

Little did they know, their encounter with the pack of wolves was just the beginning of a descent into darkness that would test their courage and resilience in ways they could scarcely imagine. But one thing was certain: they would face whatever horrors awaited them with resolute determination and unbreakable resolve.

A sense of eerie calm settled over the desolate streets as the van rumbled away, leaving the abandoned area behind. However, from the depths of the shadows cast by a nearby building, a presence stirred, and a grotesque silhouette emerged into the faint light. It moved with a sinuous grace, and its form was obscured by the cloak of darkness as it prowled with ominous intent.

With predatory precision, the creature crossed the street, its movements fluid and silent as it approached the abandoned classroom. Inside, the sedated wolf stirred, its senses slowly returning as the effects of the tranquilizer began to wane. But a sudden onslaught shattered the fragile peace before the wolf could fully regain its bearings.

In a blur of motion, the creature lunged, its massive frame pouncing upon the unsuspecting wolf with savage ferocity. With fangs bared, it descended upon its prey, tearing into its flesh with merciless abandon. Blood sprayed in crimson arcs as the creature's jaws closed around the wolf's throat, rending flesh and sinew with brutal efficiency.

The sound of ripping flesh echoed through the abandoned classroom, a grotesque symphony of violence and death. With a guttural snarl, the creature tore its victim apart, its primal instincts driving it to feast upon the helpless creature before it.

Then, with a sudden and chilling intensity, the creature drew back, its bloodied maw gaping wide as it unleashed a primal scream into the night air. The sound was both haunting and hideous, reverberating through the darkness like a harbinger of doom—a macabre announcement of its kill in a warning to any who dared challenge its reign of terror.

As the echoes of the creature's scream faded into the night, a palpable sense of dread settled over the abandoned streets, for the true horrors that lurked within the shadows had revealed themselves, and the unsuspecting inhabitants of the forsaken town could only pray for salvation from the malevolent force that now prowled among them.

"Did you hear that?" Stu's voice broke the tense silence, his eyes scanning the surrounding darkness with unease as Christina applied pressure to Heath's wound.

"Yes, it's the same sound we heard yesterday," Heath confirmed, his tone grave as he winced against the throbbing pain in his arm.

Concern etched across her features, Christina looked up at Heath, her eyes filled with worry. "How do you feel?" she inquired softly, her touch gentle as she tended to his injury.

"It's throbbing a bit, but I'll be okay," Heath reassured her, mustering a faint smile despite the discomfort. "I do have a damn headache, though." With a tender gesture, he leaned forward and pressed a kiss to Christina's forehead in a silent token of gratitude for her unwavering care.

"I have some Advil back at camp. That should help with the headache," Christina suggested in a worried voice. "And you should probably take a short nap to rest up."

Nodding in agreement, Heath acknowledged her advice, grateful for her practicality in the face of adversity. "Sounds like a plan. Monica and Jack can start their research while Willie, Stu, and I take turns keeping watch," he proposed, his gaze sweeping over the group gathered around him. "First thing in the morning, we're out of here."

"Stu, any word from Willie?" Heath's voice broke the tense silence, his gaze flicking to his teammate with concern.

Shaking his head, Stu reached for his phone, his fingers flying over the screen as he dialed Willie's number. "Willie, it's Stu. How's everything on your end?" he murmured into the receiver, his voice barely above a whisper.

A hushed reply crackled through the line and Willie's voice was strained with tension. "I'll have to get back to you," he whispered urgently, his words punctuated by the sound of rustling leaves. "A wolf is approaching our bait."

As the first wolf darted eagerly toward the lure, a second one followed, its movements cautious and deliberate as it approached the swimming pool area. Willie, his focus unwavering, took aim with precision, his finger tightening around the trigger as the carnivore neared the bait.

The tranquilizer dart found its mark with a sharp crack, striking the wolf's right shoulder with pinpoint accuracy. A yelp of pain echoed through the air as the wounded creature recoiled, its instincts driving it to flee toward the exit it had entered through.

But fate intervened as the wounded wolf collided with its companion, the force of the impact causing the second animal to turn and snap in surprise. The two creatures clashed in a frenzy of motion, their desperate attempts to escape thwarted by their collision.

Willie, Jack, and Monica watched in tense silence amid the chaos, their eyes fixed on the unfolding commotion. The trio stood ready to react as the wolves were locked in a struggle for dominance, their senses heightened by the adrenaline coursing through their veins.

The team quietly trailed the path traced by the two wolves. Their eyes caught sight of the sedated wolf sprawled on the roadway just short of reaching the outside of the swimming pool enclosure. Holding their positions for a few tense moments, they waited, ensuring the sedative took full effect before proceeding.

Once confident in their assessment, they advanced cautiously. Monica skillfully inserted a syringe, drawing out a sample of blood from the sedated wolf with practiced precision. They regrouped with the sample secured and fell in line behind Willie as he led the way back to base camp.

"Stu, it's Willie," came the call over the radio. "Sample secured. We're making our way back to camp on foot."

With the confirmation relayed, the team pressed forward, their footsteps echoing through the desolate landscape as they made their way back to the safety of their makeshift base. Each step brought them closer to their goal, yet the shadows cast by the looming darkness served as a stark reminder of the dangers that still lurked in the abandoned town.

# CHAPTER TEN

Heath stirred and gradually emerged from the depths of his restless slumber. As consciousness returned, he became aware of the dampness clinging to his skin, the sweat-soaked pillow, and the shirt that bore witness to the feverish turmoil that had gripped him in his sleep. Blinking away his haze of exhaustion, he felt the cool touch of a compress pressed against his forehead in a soothing balm against the oppressive heat that had enveloped him.

With a faint groan, he shifted, his movements drawing Christina's attention as she hovered nearby with a look of concern etched upon her features.

Sensing his awakening, she leaned in, her eyes filled with relief as she met his gaze.

“Welcome back to the land of the living,” Willie’s voice rang out from across the room, his jovial tone cutting through the somber atmosphere. Monica and Jack paused their investigation, their attention shifting to Heath as he slowly regained his bearings.

With a weak smile, Heath acknowledged his companions, gratitude mingling with exhaustion in his weary expression. Despite the trials they faced and the shadows that loomed over them, the bond of camaraderie among the team remained unbroken as a beacon of hope in the darkness that threatened to engulf them all.

“How do you feel?” a concerned Christina asked.

“A lot better now. I guess the Advil helped since my headache is also gone. My damn arm still hurts, though.

“I looked at it while you were resting,” Monica explained gently, her voice carrying a note of reassurance as she addressed Heath. “You don’t need stitches, but I administered a shot of rabies immune globulin. That provides immediate protection while the vaccine begins to take effect.”

Heath nodded, absorbing the information with a mixture of relief and gratitude. The thought of rabies, with its insidious and deadly nature, had loomed like a shadow in the back of his mind, and Monica’s swift action brought a sense of reassurance in the face of uncertainty.

"How many doses will I need?" Heath inquired, his brow furrowing with concern as he processed the gravity of the situation.

"Four doses in total," Monica replied, her tone calm and measured. "Another shot on day three, followed by one on day seven, and the final dose on day fourteen."

As Heath processed the regimen of treatments, a sense of determination settled over him. Despite the challenges that lay ahead, he knew that with the support of his team and the guidance of Monica's expertise, he would weather this trial and emerge stronger on the other side.

Heath lifted himself off his cot, his movements sluggish as he settled beside Christina, who offered him a supportive smile. With a brief glance toward Monica and Jack, who were engrossed in their examination under the microscopes, Heath couldn't help but feel a twinge of curiosity.

"Find anything interesting?" he inquired, his voice laced with anticipation as he directed his question toward the pair.

Monica looked up from her microscope, a thoughtful expression crossing her features as she considered Heath's query. "There's definitely a lot of activity in their blood," she remarked, her tone contemplative. "But we won't have any definitive findings until we can analyze the samples in our normal lab with more sophisticated equipment."

Jack nodded his agreement, his gaze focused intently on the specimen beneath his microscope. "The samples we've gathered should provide us with plenty of data to work with," he added, his voice tinged with optimism despite the inherent challenges of their current situation.

Heath nodded in understanding, a sense of excitement building within him as he awaited the results of their analysis. Though the mysteries of the samples remained shrouded in uncertainty, he couldn't shake the feeling that they were on the brink of a breakthrough—one that could potentially unravel the enigma that had brought them to this forsaken place.

"Monica now might be the time to show Heath those pictures you took at the swimming pool enclosure," Jack suggested, his voice carrying a hint of urgency as he gently pulled Monica away from her microscope.

Heath's curiosity was piqued. "What pictures?" he inquired, turning his attention to Monica as she retrieved her cellphone from her lab coat.

Monica's expression faltered momentarily before she remembered. "Oh, right," she acknowledged, a touch of embarrassment coloring her tone. Hastily, she reached into her pants pocket, retrieving the plastic baggie containing the fur and handing it over to Jack. "Here," she said, her voice a mixture of apology and anticipation. "You might want to take a look at this."

With the baggie in Jack's possession, Monica turned back to her cellphone, deftly navigating through the photos until she found the ones she was searching for. With a sense of apprehension, she presented the images to Heath while Christina hovered nearby, their collective breath held in anticipation.

As Heath's eyes scanned the photos, his expression shifted from curiosity to bewilderment. The images captured by Monica's camera revealed the eerie evidence of their encounters—the massive footprints, the strange fur—laid bare in stark detail.

Christina peered over Heath's shoulder, her breath catching in her throat as she took in the unsettling sight. The tension in the room mounted, each passing moment thick with anticipation as they waited for Heath's reaction.

Willie's voice broke the tense silence, his words laden with a sense of unease. "And, while we were setting up the bait, we stumbled upon the biggest pile of shit I've ever seen," he revealed, his tone grave as Jack and Monica nodded in solemn agreement.

Heath listened intently, his mind racing as he processed the unsettling information. A flicker of concern crossed his features as he contemplated the implications of their discoveries. "You know," he began, his voice quiet but firm, "ever since we arrived, I've had this gut instinct that we were being watched."

A ripple of unease swept through the group. He continued, his thoughts racing as he tried to make sense of the mounting evidence. "At first, I thought it was just my imagination seeing ghosts everywhere like Willie," he admitted, his words punctuated by a nervous chuckle from the group.

"Then," Heath continued, his tone sobering, "I thought it was the pack of wolves that seemed to surround us. But the size of these footprints in the photos and that pile of crap," he gestured emphatically, "seem to indicate something else is among us."

A shiver ran down Christina's back as she exchanged a wary glance with her teammates. The atmosphere in the room had shifted, the air thick with apprehension as they grappled with the unsettling realization that they were not alone in the abandoned town.

As the weight of their discovery settled upon the group like a heavy fog, Christina spoke, her voice tinged with a hint of apprehension, "Well, armed with only two dart guns, I don't suggest that we tangle with whatever it is." Her tone was laced with a touch of levity to try and ease the tension. "I say we have a nice hot meal, get some sleep, and get out of here at first light."

A murmur of agreement rippled through the room, the prospect of a warm meal and a good night's sleep offering a glimmer of comfort amid the uncertainty. Ever the pragmatist, Willie nodded in approval as he made his way to the door, his footsteps echoing through the quiet room.

"I second that idea," he declared with a wry grin, his hand resting on the doorknob as he surveyed the room. "But first, let's ensure this door and window are secure. We wouldn't want any unwelcome visitors interrupting our dinner plans."

With a collective chuckle, the group rallied around Willie, helping to fortify their makeshift sanctuary against whatever unknown threats lurked beyond. Despite the gravity of their situation, there was a sense of camaraderie—a shared resolve to face whatever challenges lay ahead with courage and determination.

And so, with the door and window securely locked or boarded up and their plans for the night settled, the group prepared for a much-needed respite from the trials of the day. Though the shadows of uncertainty loomed large, they took solace in the warmth of each other's company.

# CHAPTER ELEVEN

Christina carefully draped the large blanket over herself and Heath, who lay on his back with his good arm tucked beneath his head. Nestling close to him, she rested her head against his chest, the rhythmic beat of his heart a soothing cadence in the stillness of the night. "What do you think might be out there?" she whispered softly, her voice filled with a mixture of curiosity and apprehension.

Heath gazed up at the ceiling, his thoughts consumed by the mysteries that surrounded them. "I'm not sure," he confessed, his voice belying a sense of wonder. "This whole place is an enigma. A safety test gone wrong, an explosion spreading radiation into the atmosphere… it's like something out of a nightmare. Who knows what could be lurking in the shadows? It could be a mutant giant bear for all we know."

As Christina pondered his words in thoughtful silence, Heath ran his hand gently under her blouse, the warmth of her skin igniting a spark of desire within him. Feeling his touch, she reciprocated, her hand tracing a path down his chest until it reached his waiting arousal. "Someone must be feeling better," she teased, a mischievous glint dancing in her eyes. "We'll have to be quiet."

With practiced ease, they shed their clothing beneath the shelter of the blanket, their movements slow and deliberate as they sought to maintain the illusion of tranquility in the face of mounting passion. Their lips met in a tender embrace, the kiss soft and sweet in a silent communion of desire and longing.

Christina straddled Heath, her body arching toward him as he entered her, their movements synchronized in a dance of ecstasy. Heat and pleasure washed over them, their shared passion building to a crescendo as they surrendered to the primal rhythm of their desires.

In the hushed stillness of the night, they found solace in each other's arms, their bodies entwined in a symphony of sensation. And as they succumbed to the blissful release of their climaxes, they knew that no matter what terrors awaited them in the darkness, they would face them together, united in their love and strength.

Christina and Heath lay entwined beneath the blanket as the night wore on, and their breathing was slow and steady as they drifted into a peaceful slumber. However, their rest was short-lived, shattered by the sudden cacophony of hideous growls echoing through the camp and filling the air with primal terror.

They were jolted instantly awake, their senses on high alert as they realized they were not alone. Willie sprang into action with a surge of adrenaline, his massive frame moving swiftly to barricade the door, his sheer strength holding it steady against the relentless assault from outside while Monica and Christina screamed.

Meanwhile, Jack and Stu rushed to reinforce the defenses, hastily placing sharp boards next to the already boarded-up broken window. Tan, their ever-vigilant lookout, stood poised to alert the group of any further threats, his eyes scanning the darkness for signs of danger.

The attack intensified as the sound of splintering wood reverberated through the air. The lifeforms outside pressed forward with renewed ferocity. Part of the wooden door, protected by Willie's formidable strength, began to buckle under the relentless onslaught, inching closer to collapse with each passing moment.

Desperate to stem the tide of the onslaught, Heath took aim with his dart gun, his hands steady despite the chaos unfolding around him. With a swift motion, he fired a dart through a narrow opening in the door, the sharp hiss of the tranquilizer punctuating the night air.

A shrill scream pierced the darkness, followed by the attack's sudden cessation as the creatures outside recoiled from the tranquilizer's effects. For a fleeting moment, silence descended upon the camp, broken only by the ragged breaths of the weary defenders as they dared to hope the worst was over.

As the first light of dawn seeped over the horizon, painting the camp in eerie shadows, the group huddled together, their faces drawn with exhaustion and fear. A sense of unease was everywhere, casting a shadow over their tenuous feelings of relief.

"What do we do now?" Willie's voice cut through the quiet, his tone laced with apprehension. "That was no damn pack of wolves."

Heath nodded solemnly, his mind racing as he tried to make sense of the night's harrowing events. "You're right, Willie," he agreed, his voice hushed with dread. "What I saw outside the door before I fired that shot… it was like nothing I've ever seen before."

His words lingered as each syllable weighed heavy with implications. "It had to have been over seven feet tall," Heath continued, his voice trembling with fear. "And it was covered in fur. Its hands were massive, with claws larger than any bear I've ever encountered."

Christina listened to Heath's description, her heart hammering in her chest with each terrifying detail.

The realization dawned upon them like a cold chill, sinking deep into their bones: they were not dealing with mere animals but something far more sinister and malevolent.

The group exchanged anxious glances with the specter of the unknown looming over them, their minds racing with the uncertainty of their next move. They knew they could not stay in this place for long in the face of such unimaginable horror, but where could they go? And what other terrors awaited them beyond the safety of their makeshift sanctuary?

They had long determined their cellphones were useless. There was no way to call for help. A sense of foreboding settled over the group as they grappled with these challenges, the fear of the unknown looming large in their hearts. In the desolate wasteland of Chernobyl's abandoned town, the line between life and death had blurred beyond recognition, and the true horrors of the night had only just begun to reveal themselves.

"Sorry, guys. I'm not feeling well. I think I need to lay down and take another nap," Heath said, woozy on his feet. Christina helped him to the cot where they had slept the night before.

"You wanted to see us?" Ivan asked, his voice tinged with a hint of trepidation as he and Yuri entered their supervisor's office.

"Yes, have a seat," the supervisor replied, gesturing towards the chairs opposite his desk. "When you went on patrol last night, how did you find the scientists inside Containment Zone #2?"

Ivan exchanged a nervous glance with Yuri, their guilty consciences weighing heavily upon them. "Um, I guess they were… fine," Yuri finally stammered out, speaking for both.

The supervisor raised an eyebrow, his expression unreadable as he considered Yuri's response. "I see. And are they making any progress on their research? They're supposed to leave the area today."

Ivan shrugged helplessly, a sheepish grin spreading across his face. "Well, you see, we're not exactly scientists," he admitted with a self-deprecating chuckle. "They had loads of equipment when they arrived, though! We watched them unload their stuff and wished them luck."

Their supervisor regarded them with a mixture of exasperation and amusement before delivering his next statement. "The home office received a call late last night. They're concerned because their employees aren't answering their radios or cellphones."

Ivan felt a bead of sweat trickle down his forehead, his nerves kicking into overdrive as he braced himself for what was coming next. "Um, right," he mumbled, his voice barely audible over his heart's pounding.

"Never mind," the supervisor said with a resigned sigh. "I want the two of you to head out there now. Tell the scientists to answer their damn cellphones and remind them they're supposed to leave the area immediately. Stay out there until they do. Do you understand?"

Ivan and Yuri nodded in unison, relief flooding through them as they scrambled to comply with their supervisor's orders. As they hurried out of the office, they exchanged a glance, sharing a silent vow to never let their patrol duties slip again. After all, when it came to dereliction of duty, they had learned their lesson the hard way.

# CHAPTER TWELVE

"I thought he had our asses," Yuri muttered under his breath as he settled into the driver's seat of the security truck, his relief palpable. "Fucking scientists. Let Chernobyl decay for all I care."

Ivan nodded in agreement as he climbed into the passenger seat beside Yuri, his anxiety beginning to dissipate. "Yeah, when he started asking about how they were doing, I almost shit my pants. Thank God he didn't interrogate us further," he confessed, his tone laden with gratitude. "Now we can go out there and order them out of the area. We'll write up a complete report showing we did our job."

Yuri chuckled dryly as he started the engine, the air filling with the sound of the truck rumbling to life. "Don't worry, I've got the vodka right here," he replied, patting his jacket pocket where the bottle lay concealed. "Nothing like a little liquid courage to get us through this."

Ivan and Yuri exchanged smirks, the tension of their earlier encounter slowly fading into the background. As they drove toward Containment Zone #2, their thoughts turned to the task ahead. They were determined to assert their authority and ensure the scientists complied with their orders.

And as the miles stretched out before them, they couldn't help but feel a sense of camaraderie in the face of adversity, united in their mission to maintain order in the desolate wasteland of Chernobyl. With the bottle of vodka tucked safely between them, they were ready to face whatever challenges lay ahead, armed with determination and a healthy dose of liquid courage.

"Why don't you turn some music on and none of that Taylor Swift crap," Ivan requested with a hint of irritation as they cruised down the deserted road. Yuri complied, fiddling with the radio dial in search of a channel they could both agree upon.

However, before they could settle on a station, Yuri's hand froze on the dial as he slammed on the brakes, the screech of rubber against asphalt echoing through the truck's cab. The vehicle lurched to a stop with a jolt, the sudden impact sending them both lurching forward in their seats. A thud reverberated inside the cab with an unmistakable sound; they had hit something.

Cursing under their breaths, Ivan and Yuri quickly scrambled out of the truck, their hearts racing as they surveyed the scene before them. A huge dent marred the front of the vehicle, the metal twisted and mangled, with traces of fur and blood smeared across the surface.

Their eyes widened in horror as they followed the trail of destruction, their gazes coming to rest upon a set of large footprints imprinted in the dirt. The realization dawned upon them like a cold chill: whatever they had hit was no ordinary creature.

As they compared notes of what they had seen before the impact, a sense of dread settled over them like a suffocating blanket. Yuri, the driver, recalled with chilling clarity the image of a huge hairy creature darting across the road in front of them, its massive form moving with unnatural speed.

"It ran on all fours at first," Yuri recounted, his voice trembling with fear. "But then, after the impact, it stood up on two legs and disappeared into the darkness."

Ivan's blood ran cold as he absorbed Yuri's words, the weight of their encounter sinking in with bone-chilling certainty. They knew, at that moment, that they were not alone in the desolate wilderness of Chernobyl. And as they stared into the darkness beyond, they couldn't help but wonder what other horrors lurked in the shadows, waiting to reveal themselves.

"Fuck! Fuck!" shouted Ivan, his voice tinged with frustration as he surveyed the damage to the truck. "We just avoided getting our butts fired, and now look at this piece of shit." He kicked the side of the truck near the dent, his anger boiling over.

"Calm down, my friend," Yuri said, his tone soothing as he handed Ivan the vodka. "We are not the only ones who have had run-ins with mutant wolves or deer out here, da? By the time we contact those scientists, watch them leave, and return to headquarters, it will be dark. We tell the boss the truth or a version of the truth. We say a large deer ran out of the forest, and we could not avoid it. No reason to tell him what you really saw, right? Sure, he will be pissed, but what can he say? Accidents happen."

"You're right," Ivan conceded, taking a sip of vodka and feeling some of his tension melt away. "As they say in that movie Forrest Gump, shit happens." They both laughed, the tension of the moment momentarily forgotten.

Unbeknownst to them, a creature lurked in the shadows of the forest, its eyes gleaming with malevolence as it watched the two men. Licking its wound, it waited patiently, its hunger for vengeance simmering beneath the surface. As Ivan and Yuri continued their conversation, oblivious to the danger that lurked nearby, they had no idea their encounter with the mutant creature was far from over.

"Okay, let's go and order those researchers out of here," Ivan said as the two walked back to their damaged truck.

"We wait until the sun is completely up so we can see our surroundings," Heath said to the attentive group, his voice urgent. "Due to the size of the creature I shot, I don't know if the sedatives will be effective, and he was not alone." He looked around the room, his eyes searching for signs of understanding among his companions.

"Here is what we will do," he continued, his mind racing with plans to ensure their safety. "Take the wood from all that broken-down furniture over there and start sharpening them into pointed stakes. A spear is better than nothing."

Christina nodded in agreement; her eyes were filled with determination. "And make torches," she added, her voice firm and resolute.

"Exactly," Heath affirmed, grateful for her quick thinking. "I don't know of any animal that is not afraid of fire. Tan, you and Stu load up only the vital equipment, especially the vials of blood. I want everything packed and ready to go with us as we run to the van," but before he could finish his instructions, a sudden wave of pain engulfed him, sending him reeling.

Heath's hands flew to his ears, his screams piercing the air as agony ripped through his skull. The group watched in horror as he began to thrash around in circles, his movements erratic and frenzied. Monica's cries joined his, her confusion mirroring that of the rest of the group.

"What's wrong with Heath?" Monica cried out, her voice filled with panic. Christina reached out to him in a gesture of comfort and concern, but he slapped her hand away, his focus consumed by his torment. Desperate and helpless, he clawed at his arms and legs, his skin raw and bloody from the strength of his scratching.

With mounting dread, the group realized that something was terribly wrong with their leader, but as they stood frozen in shock and disbelief, they had no idea how to help him or what had triggered this sudden and terrifying transformation. As Heath's screams echoed through the room, they could only watch in horror, praying for a solution to their nightmare.

"Could he be reacting to the injection you gave him?" Willie's voice trembled with concern as he turned to look at Monica, his eyes wide with worry.

"No, there is no chance that is what is causing this," Monica replied firmly, her brow furrowed with determination. She wasted no time in acting, swiftly grabbing one of the darts and carefully extracting some of the sedative solution from the small container.

With practiced precision, she loaded the dart into a gun and, without hesitation, fired it at Heath. The effects were almost immediate; the sedative took hold and caused him to become woozy. With Willie's help, they gently guided him to his cot, laying him down with care.

Christina's panic was evident as she watched the scene unfold before her. "What did you do to him? You killed him," she exclaimed, her voice rising in hysteria.

"No, I didn't," Monica reassured her, her tone calm and steady despite the chaos around them. "I drastically reduced the amount of sedative in the dart to much less than what we used on the wolves. He should be out for about 20-30 minutes. I suggest we use some of our blankets to secure him. He may wake up in the same condition or worse."

As Monica's words sank in, the group exchanged uneasy glances. With Heath now temporarily subdued, they knew that they had to act quickly to ensure their safety and uncover the cause of his sudden affliction. As they huddled together, their minds racing with possibilities, they braced themselves for the challenges that lay ahead, knowing their ordeal was far from over.

"Alright, everyone, listen up," Christina's voice cut through the tension, commanding attention from the group. "We need to carry out what Heath told us to do. Weapons, torches. Tan, you watch the door. Willie, before you help us make weapons, point a few spears at that window and brace them in case they try to rush us. Let's go, people!"

Her words spurred them into action, igniting a sense of urgency as they scrambled to gather makeshift weapons and torches. Tan stationed himself by the door, his eyes scanning the room for any signs of danger, while Willie quickly moved to fortify the window, his movements swift and purposeful.

With adrenaline coursing through their veins, they worked together determinedly, their focus singular as they prepared for whatever threat lurked beyond the safety of their makeshift stronghold. Spears were sharpened, torches were fashioned, and every available resource was harnessed in their fight for survival.

They readied themselves for the unknown with unwavering resolve fueled by the knowledge that their lives depended on their readiness and unity. As they stood poised on the brink of danger, they knew they would face whatever came their way with courage and fortitude, united in their commitment to overcome the darkness that surrounded them.

# CHAPTER THIRTEEN

"That's strange," Ivan remarked, his brow furrowing as he peered out at the abandoned vans. "Looks like the vans haven't moved."

Yuri nodded, his expression grim. "Yeah, and no one is walking around. That's okay. Park over there, and let's get out and scare them out of here," he said with an air of authority, his voice laced with determination.

As they approached the vans, a sense of unease settled over them, their footsteps echoing in the eerie silence of the abandoned town. The atmosphere was thick with tension, and each passing moment was fraught with uncertainty.

They purposefully parked the truck and stepped out onto the desolate street, their eyes scanning the area for any signs of movement. But the silence remained unbroken, the only sound the rustling of leaves in the breeze.

As they advanced cautiously, a nagging sense of foreboding gnawed at the edges of their minds. Something wasn't right, and they both felt it deep in their bones. However, they pressed on with nerves of steel and determination in their hearts, determined to uncover the truth behind the mystery that lay before them.

"Hello, inside the building. Security," Ivan's voice echoed through the empty corridors. His words were met with silence. Undeterred, he exchanged a glance with Yuri, a silent signal passing between them.

"Hello! This is security. We are coming in," Yuri announced, his voice firm as he nodded to Ivan to lead the way. They advanced toward the entrance with cautious steps, their flashlights cutting through the darkness like beacons of hope. But still, there was no response, only the eerie silence of the abandoned building.

As they crossed the threshold, a foul stench assaulted their senses, causing Yuri to wrinkle his nose in disgust. "Shit, what is that smell?" he exclaimed, his voice tinged with revulsion.

"You answered your own question, I think. It smells like shit," Ivan replied dryly, his gaze sweeping the area as they surveyed their surroundings. Yuri followed his lead, his flashlight illuminating the ground where a pool of blood had gathered, dark and ominous against the floor.

"Looks like blood, and lots of it," Yuri observed, his voice grim as they turned a corner and entered the main room. Their eyes widened in horror as they took in the remnants of a gruesome massacre laid bare.

"Stop!" Ivan's command cut through the silence, his flashlight trembling slightly as it swept along the floor. Ivan and Yuri stood frozen in horror as they surveyed the scene before them. The housing unit within Containment Zone #2 was supposed to be a safe place for the scientists to conduct their research. Instead, it had become a chamber of nightmares. The walls were splattered with blood, and the air was thick with the metallic tang of death. Bodies lay strewn across the floor, torn apart with savage brutality. The once sterile corridors were now painted with the remains of a grim struggle.

Yuri's stomach churned, bile rising in his throat as he struggled to comprehend the carnage before him. "What… what could have done this?" he muttered, his voice barely audible.

Ivan shook his head, his hands trembling as he gripped his weapon tighter. "I don't know, maybe mutant wolves, but we need to get out of here. Now."

As they turned to leave, the sound of other footsteps echoed through the corridor. The steps created vibrations even on the concrete flooring. Instinctively, they raised their weapons, their hearts pounding in their chests. Nothing could have prepared them for what emerged from the shadows.

The creatures stood over seven feet tall, their bodies hulking and twisted, resembling wolves walking upright on two legs. Their eyes glowed with an unnatural hunger, and their razor-sharp claws dripped with fresh blood. Saliva dripped to their chest. Ivan and Yuri opened fire, emptying their handguns in a desperate attempt to fend off the advancing horde.

Their efforts were futile. The creatures moved with uncanny speed, closing the distance between them in seconds. With a ferocious snarl, they lunged forward, tearing into flesh and bone with savage precision. Ivan and Yuri screamed in agony as the creatures ripped them apart, their desperate cries echoing along the desolate halls of Containment Zone #2.

As the last vestiges of life faded from their broken bodies, the creatures turned their attention back to the bloody feast that lay before them, their hunger insatiable and their thirst for blood unquenchable.

# CHAPTER FOURTEEN

A pile of crudely fashioned weapons lay at the center of the room, just visible in the dim light. They were a stark contrast to the pristine research equipment carefully arranged in a corner near the exit door by Stu and Tan. The group's attention shifted to Heath as he began to stir, his movements tentative as he pulled at his restraints.

"What is this? Untie me," Heath demanded, his voice urgent.

Christina rushed to his side, her brow furrowed with concern as she knelt beside his cot. "Heath, you're not well," she began, her voice gentle but firm. "You totally freaked us all out, screaming and thrashing about. Monica had to sedate you. Do you remember any of that?"

Heath's brow creased in confusion as he struggled to piece together the events that had transpired. Memories flashed through his mind like fragments of a shattered mirror, disjointed and hazy. He recalled the overwhelming sense of panic that had engulfed him, the primal urge to break free from an unseen force gripping him in its clutches. Beyond that, the details remained elusive, lost in a fog of uncertainty.

"I… I don't know," he murmured, his voice barely above a whisper. "Everything is… blurry."

As the seriousness of his condition settled over them like a heavy shroud, the group exchanged worried glances, their concern palpable in the air. Heath's sudden deterioration had cast a shadow of fear over their already precarious situation, leaving them grappling with the unsettling realization that their struggle for survival had only just begun.

Christina was the first to spot a tuft of unruly hair sprouting from beneath Heath's t-shirt and nestled on his shoulder. Hastily, she covered it with her hand, hoping to shield it from anyone else's notice. Her gaze then fixated on Heath's eyes, noticing a subtle shift in their hue, as if his irises were undergoing a transformation.

Heath met Christina's gaze and flashed her a smile. She observed his canine teeth, which seemed to have elongated and become more pronounced. Strangely,

Heath appeared oblivious to the changes manifesting in his body.

"Listen up, everyone!" Willie's voice cut through the tense air, commanding attention as he approached the broken, boarded-up window. "Do you hear that? Does it sound like gunshots?"

In the distance, the sound of rapid gunfire pierced the stillness, echoing through the desolate surroundings. However, as quickly as it began, the barrage ceased, leaving behind an eerie silence.

"It could be the Ukrainian government! They might be coming to our rescue," Monica exclaimed, her voice ringing with hope and excitement. The prospect of salvation flickered in the dim light of their despair, igniting a spark of optimism among the group.

With newfound determination, they scrambled to devise a plan, their minds racing with possibilities. They knew they had to seize this opportunity to draw attention to their hidden refuge, to signal their presence amidst the chaos of the outside world.

"We have to make ourselves seen and heard," Willie declared, his eyes alight with determination. "It's our only chance to get out of here alive."

They set to work urgently, gathering whatever makeshift tools and materials they could find to create a beacon of hope amid the surrounding darkness. Each nail hammered and each board removed brought them one step closer to the possibility of salvation.

As they worked tirelessly to make their presence known, their hearts swelled with anticipation, daring to believe that help was finally within reach. But amid the glimmer of hope, a lingering fear gnawed at their collective minds. Would their efforts be enough to attract their would-be saviors, or would they remain trapped in this nightmare, forever lost to the horrors of the unknown?

"Alright, listen up," Willie's voice carried a sense of urgency as he outlined his plan. "We need to act fast. We'll haul these boards outside and siphon some gas from the van. Then, we'll douse the boards, light 'em up, and let the smoke do the rest. It'll be like a beacon for the Ukrainian troops, guiding them straight to us."

His words lingered ominously in the air, the danger pressing down upon them like a weight. However, Willie's plan offered a glimmer of hope amid the chaos and uncertainty – a chance, however slim, to break free from the suffocating grip of their confinement.

They set to work with a shared sense of determination, their movements quick and purposeful as they dragged the pile of boards outside and retrieved the necessary supplies from the van. Each step brought them closer to their goal, their hearts pounding with anticipation as they prepared to ignite their makeshift signal.

Stu siphoned a cup of gasoline from the van's tank and poured the liquid onto the wood in scattered locations.

As the flames licked hungrily at the gas-soaked wood, a plume of thick, black smoke billowed into the sky, twisting and spiraling against the desolate landscape's backdrop. It was a beacon of desperation, a plea for salvation amid the vast expanse of uncertainty that stretched out before them.

As they watched the smoke rise into the air, their hearts swelled with a mixture of fear and hope, knowing their fate now lay in the hands of the unknown. Would their signal be seen? Would help arrive in time to rescue them from their captors' clutches? Only time would tell as they waited with bated breath for the sound of approaching footsteps, praying for deliverance from the nightmare that had become their reality.

# CHAPTER FIFTEEN

"Why aren't they coming to rescue us?" Monica's voice trembled, tears welling in her eyes. "Surely they must see the smoke from our fire."

Willie glanced toward the horizon; his brow was furrowed with concern. "Perhaps they're still engaged in combat with those creatures elsewhere in the housing project. They'll come for us as soon as they can."

Tan shook his head, his expression grim. "I wish I could share your optimism, but if the military was actively exterminating these abominations, we would have heard the thunderous roar of gunfire by now. It should echo like a war zone." He scanned the desolate landscape, a sense of dread settling over him like a suffocating fog.

"I think I might have a solution," Stu proposed, his eyes alight with determination. "That fire won't sustain us indefinitely, but if I fetch the spare tire from the van and toss it onto the flames, it'll produce thick, billowing smoke that'll last far longer."

Monica's gaze flickered with a glimmer of hope as she considered the plan. "But won't burning rubber release toxic fumes?"

Stu nodded, acknowledging the concern. "It's a risk we'll have to take. Right now, our priority is attracting attention and getting rescued. Besides, smoke from burning rubber will be unmistakable."

"Frankly, I couldn't care less about toxic smoke and saving the planet," Tan declared, his tone edged with frustration. "All I want is for us to get out of here alive."

Monica placed a comforting hand on Tan's shoulder, her expression sympathetic. "You're right. I'm sorry, Tan. Survival comes first."

Willie nodded in agreement. "We'll deal with the consequences later. Right now, we must focus on finding a way out of this nightmare."

Stu glanced around at the desolate landscape, a flicker of determination in his eyes. "Let's not lose hope. We'll find a way to make it out of here together."

Willie nodded in agreement. "It's worth a shot. Let's do it."

With a shared sense of urgency, they sprang into action, each member of the group playing a vital role in executing Stu's plan.

"I'll take point with my spear. Stu, stick close to me," Willie commanded, his voice firm with resolve. "We don't know how many of those things are out there, but we know it's more than one. Use the key fob to ensure the van is unlocked before we reach it. Grab the tire, roll it to the bonfire, and hustle our asses back here as fast as we can. Understand?"

Stu nodded; his jaw was set with determination. "Got it, Willie. I'll be right behind you."

Willie and Stu stepped cautiously out of the relative safety of their shelter, finding the air thick with tension and their senses heightened by the imminent danger lurking in the shadows. Willie gripped his spear tightly, his muscles tense as he scanned the darkness for any sign of movement.

Stu hurried to the van, fumbling with the key fob as adrenaline surged through his veins. The van's doors unlocked with a click, and he swung them open. The interior was bathed in dim light from the moon above. He reached for the spare tire, his fingers trembling with urgency, and dragged it onto the gravel-strewn ground.

However, as Stu heaved the tire toward the crackling bonfire, a low, guttural growl echoed through the night, sending a shiver down his spine. Willie's head snapped around, his eyes widening in alarm as he spotted dark, looming figures emerging from the shadows, their eyes gleaming with hunger.

"We've got company!" Willie shouted, his shrill voice cutting through the stillness of the night.

Heart pounding, Stu abandoned the tire and sprinted back toward Willie, his breath coming in ragged gasps. Together, they raced toward the safety of their shelter, the sound of heavy footsteps pounding behind them.

Just as they reached the building's relative security, a deafening crash echoed through the pre-dawn light as one of the creatures smashed through the boarded-up window where Tan was stationed. Its hideous hairy arms and long-clawed fingers dug into Tan's chest and neck. The air filled with the sickening stench of blood and gore as the creature dragged a screaming Tan out into the darkness, leaving a trail of crimson in its wake.

Terror and helplessness washed over Willie and Stu as they watched in horror, their breath catching in their throats. Then, amid the chaos and despair, a plume of black smoke rose from the tire, casting an eerie glow over the scene. It was a grim reminder of the desperate hope that had driven them to risk it all in the face of unimaginable terror.

"Quick! Help me board up that window again," Willie urged, his voice strained with urgency. "Christina, bring me some more spears so we can secure it better."

Christina and Monica were lost in a frenzy of panic, their screams piercing the air as terror gripped them. Ignoring Willie's command, they seemed oblivious to the imminent danger that lurked just beyond their shelter's fragile barrier.

"Christina! Snap out of it!" Willie's voice rose above the chaos, commanding attention. "We're vulnerable, and we must secure that window."

Finally, Christina shook herself from the grip of fear, her eyes wide with alarm as she registered Willie's words. With a sense of determination, she rallied, joining forces with Monica and Stu to gather whatever makeshift weapons they could find.

As they hurried to reinforce the window, their hands trembling with adrenaline, they placed various sharpened pieces of wood and debris, their hearts pounding with the knowledge that their very survival depended on the strength of their makeshift barricade. Each plank hammered into place was a desperate attempt to keep the horrors of the night at bay in testament to their unwavering determination to defy the darkness that threatened to consume them.

"Do you think they'll attack again?" Stu's voice trembled with anxiety as he turned to Willie for reassurance.

Willie's expression was grim as he surveyed their fragile sanctuary, his eyes shadowed with apprehension. "I have no doubt," he replied, his voice barely above a whisper. "The bigger question is how long can we hold them off for."

His gaze shifted to Monica and Christina, who sat huddled together in a corner, their faces etched with fear and exhaustion. "Look at them," he continued, his tone heavy with concern. "They're at their wits' end. If any of those creatures manage to breach our defenses, they won't be any help to us."

A deep sigh escaped Willie as he glanced toward Heath, who lay motionless on a makeshift cot, his pallor growing increasingly ashen with each passing moment. "And as for Heath," he murmured, his voice tinged with sorrow, "have you seen him? He's not getting better; he's getting worse."

# CHAPTER SIXTEEN

As the somber atmosphere enveloped them like a heavy shroud, Monica busied herself with brewing coffee in a feeble attempt to provide some semblance of comfort in the wake of Tan's untimely demise. Each member of the group grappled with their grief in their own way, their hearts heavy with the weight of loss.

Christina tenderly placed another damp cloth on Heath's forehead, her movements gentle and comforting as she tried to alleviate his suffering. Heath offered her a weak smile, a glimmer of gratitude shining in his eyes.

"How do you feel?" Christina's voice was soft and concerned as she leaned in closer.

Heath's response was tentative, his words uncertain. "A little better, I think. The headache's gone." Christina reached out to stroke his hand, and the warmth of her touch was a balm to his weary soul.

At that moment, Christina's gaze lingered on Heath's hand, a sudden realization dawning on her. She had never paid much attention to his fingers before, even during their most intimate moments, but now, she couldn't help but notice how long and slender they were, with nails in bad need of a trim. It was a detail that had previously escaped her notice.

Before she could dwell further on her newfound observation, Heath's sudden movement snapped her back to reality. With a start, he sat up, his eyes wide with alarm.

"Do you hear that? They're coming," Heath exclaimed, his voice filled with urgency.

The group's attention shifted to Heath, their senses sharpened by the looming threat that hung over them like a dark cloud. Willie and Stu hastened to peer through the cracks in the door and window, scanning the desolate landscape for any sign of movement.

"I don't see any movement," Stu reported, his voice tense with apprehension.

"Me either," Willie confirmed, his brow furrowed with concern. He turned his gaze to Heath and Christina, worry etched on his features. "Is he hallucinating? Maybe he's running a fever."

The air was thick with tension as they grappled with the uncertainty of their situation, their nerves frayed by the relentless onslaught of danger that seemed to close in on them from all sides.

Christina pressed her hand against Heath's forehead, relieved to find his temperature within normal range. "What did you hear?" she asked with concern.

Heath's panic escalated as he exclaimed, "You guys don't hear it? They're coming from all sides. There are at least eight of them!"

The urgency in Heath's voice sent a chill down their spines, each member of the group exchanging worried glances as they strained to hear what he was describing. Willie and Stu peered outside once more, their senses on high alert, but saw nothing amiss.

Willie shook his head in disbelief. "He must be hallucinating," he concluded, his tone skeptical. "Either that or his hearing is far better than mine." Willie reached down and grabbed his cup of coffee. He took a sip and returned his attention to the crack in the door. He was shocked at what he saw.

"Get ready! Here they come!" Willie's voice shattered the tense silence, sending shockwaves of terror through Christina and Monica, their screams echoing in the claustrophobic confines of their shelter. Stu's grip tightened on his spear, knuckles whitening with fear, mirroring Willie's grim determination.

As the first ghastly shadows loomed outside, Willie, Stu, and Jack braced themselves, their spears poised to strike at the first sign of danger. Christina and Monica, their faces pale with dread, seized makeshift weapons and positioned themselves beside their comrades, their hearts hammering in their chests.

The creatures descended upon them with a deafening crash, launching a coordinated assault on the door and window simultaneously. The flimsy barricades offered little resistance as grotesque hands and arms thrust through the cracks, their twisted forms contorted with malevolent intent.

But Willie, Christina, Monica, Jack, and Stu refused to yield to the encroaching horror. They lunged forward out of primal instinct and sheer desperation, their weapons finding their marks with deadly precision. The air was thick with the sickening stench of decay as the creatures howled in agony, their grotesque forms writhing in pain.

With each stab and thrust, they forced the abominations back, their collective resolve unyielding in the face of overwhelming terror. Blood mingled with sweat as they fought for their very survival, the battle raging on in a frenzy of violence and desperation.

Finally, with a collective roar of defiance, they drove the creatures back, their assailants retreating into the darkness from whence they came. Breathing heavily, their bodies trembled with exhaustion and adrenaline. Willie, Christina, Monica, Jack, and Stu stood victorious, their spirits battered but unbroken by the horrors they had faced.

But as they caught their breath, they knew that even with the sun starting to rise, it was far from over, and the shadows still held untold terrors waiting to descend upon them once more. With grim determination, they braced themselves for the next onslaught, knowing that their fight for survival had only just begun.

"Well, we know one thing," Jack remarked, his voice edged with unease. "These things aren't afraid of sunlight. Since we can't see them now, either they've retreated back into the forest or sought refuge in other abandoned buildings."

Willie nodded in agreement, his mind racing with strategies to combat the relentless threat they faced. "You're right. These creatures aren't deterred by darkness or light, but I think Monica and Christina need to make some more torches. The next time they stick their damned arms inside, we burn them."

As if spurred into action by Willie's directive, Monica and Christina wasted no time in gathering materials to fashion new torches, their movements swift and purposeful amidst the tension that filled the room.

"What do you think those things are?" Jack's voice trembled slightly as he voiced the question that lingered in all their minds. "They walk upright like humans, but they also move like four-legged animals. And their hair… it's reminiscent of the wolves we encountered, but their ears, claws, and fangs… they're far more menacing. And they are intelligent. Look at the way they attacked. Not just a frontal assault but also hitting us in our two vulnerable points."

The group fell into a heavy silence, each member grappling with the unsettling implications of Jack's observations. The mere thought of the creatures sent shivers down their spines, a collective fear that united them in their shared struggle against the encroaching darkness.

As the hours passed without a second assault, Christina took it upon herself to tend to the group's needs. Heath had fallen back to sleep, his rest interrupted by fitful dreams and feverish mutterings. With a sense of purpose, she gathered food and began distributing it to the others, her movements methodical as she sought to provide a small semblance of normalcy amid the chaos that surrounded them.

Amid her tasks, Christina stumbled upon a book Jack had referred to earlier, its pages worn with age and filled with tales of the Chernobyl disaster. As she flipped through the pages, her eyes alighted on a chapter titled, 'What happened to the people who were evacuated from Pripyat, Ukraine after the Chernobyl meltdown? Are any of them still alive?'

Intrigued, Christina delved into the text, absorbing the grim details of the aftermath of the disaster. The words painted a stark picture of the lives torn asunder by the ravages of radiation and displacement, the trauma and hardship etched into the very fabric of their existence.

She paused as she reached a passage that had been underlined, her heart skipping a beat as she read the words once more. "Some people have returned to their homes in the exclusion zone despite the risks, as they have strong emotional ties to the area and have been able to find ways to make a living there."

A chilling realization washed over Christina as she considered the possibility that the creatures they were battling could be mutated remnants of those who had chosen to return to the contaminated lands. The thought sent a shudder down her spine; it was a sobering reminder of the horrors that lurked in the shadows of the past, waiting to reclaim their lost souls.

# CHAPTER SEVENTEEN

Christina's voice cut through the tense silence, commanding the group's attention as she read the sentence underlined in Jack's book aloud. "Some people have returned to their homes in the exclusion zone despite the risks, as they had strong emotional ties to the area and have found ways to make a living there." As the weight of her words settled over them, a murmur of uncertainty rippled through the group.

"Yeah, I remember underlining that," Jack admitted, his brow furrowing in thought. "I couldn't help but wonder what tests had been done on them. Monica and I theorized that if the mutant wolves really had built up resistance to cancer, what about those who returned to the contamination zones?"

The implications of his question caused each member of the group to grapple with the unsettling possibility that the creatures they were facing could be the twisted result of human exposure to radiation. The thought sent chills down their spines in a stark reminder of the ever-present dangers that lurked in the aftermath of the Chernobyl disaster.

Christina puts the book down. "Maybe these creatures we are fighting are mutated remnants of those who had chosen to return to the contaminated zones. No one spoke until Monica interjected her feelings.

"Yes. Think about it. It's quite logical when you consider it. Picture this: these beings move on all fours yet possess the remarkable ability to stand upright like humans. Not only that, but they also possess intelligence, a blend of wolf-like instincts intertwined with distinctly human qualities."

Jack leaned forward. "So, like the mutant wolves, these are former residents who decided to stay or return to the contamination zones and have mutated into those things outside."

"That does make sense, but how does that help us?" Willie asked.

Christina looks at the group. "Did you guys see that movie where Vikings tracked down the hiding place of what they thought were bears?"

"Yeah. I saw that. They decided that since the creatures they were fighting dressed and act liked bears, the question was where do bears live." Willie replied.

"Exactly," and excited Christina continued. "And they determined caves. The creatures we're up against, unlike the movie, don't think they are wolves; they've evolved into something far more advanced within their species."

"I think I follow," Stu says. "So, the question is where would they hang out, assuming they do together?"

"Well. They act like wolves, so where do wolves hand out?" Monica asks.

"Wolves travel in packs and live in dens. So, all we have to do is find their den. You're talking about taking the fight to them." Willie replied.

"Wait a minute. Even if our theory is right, and we somehow luck out and find their den, what do we do then? Shoot as many as we can with two dart guns, hoping they stand in line to be shot?" Jack inquired. No one spoke seeking answers internally.

"Before they attack again, Jack, you and I need to do a complete workup of the blood samples we have. We need to find their weakness. It will be up to you Willie and Stu, to think about where these assholes are hiding," Monica said, as she returned to her workstation and began looking into her microscope.

"What about me?" a helpless Christina asked.

"You need to care for Heath," Willie answered. "To me, he is getting worse so we need to get out of here and get him to a hospital."

As they pondered the implications of their theory of the creatures, a sense of unease settled over them, casting a shadow over their already precarious situation. With each passing moment, the realization dawned that they were not just battling creatures that roamed the desolate landscape but also ghosts of the past who haunted the very fabric of their existence.

"What do you think about this?" Willie asked. "Another assault is imminent. When they do, and assuming we hold them off again, we shoot one of them with the tranquilizer gun. Heath already said that he wasn't sure if the dosage would be enough to completely sedate the beasts, but that is all we need; partial sedation."

Stu, looking puzzled, raises his hand like in a school classroom. "I don't follow. You want to shoot one of the creatures knowing it might not be enough to put it down. How does that help?"

"We pick one of the beast while holding the rest back. If we hold off the horde, they will retreat. The partially sedated one should be easy to follow back to their den," Willie answered.

"Ah, now I follow you. But that is going to be risky if we run into a group of them out in the open."

Willie shrugs his shoulders. "We are running out of options." He has everyone's attention.

"Stu and I will come up with a plan on how to track down the creatures and find their hide out. Assuming they act like a pack of wolves, we will shoot one of them during their next attack."

"You think they are coming back?" Monica asks nervously.

"I have no doubt. As we hold them off with spears and you and Christina burn their arms and hands, I will shoot one of them."

"But Heath already said, he is not sure how powerful the sedative in a dart will be against a creature that big and tall," Christina said.

Willie looked at Christina and the group before answering. "I understand. But that could work in our advantage."

Jack looked confused. "I don't follow."

"We are hoping that the sedative is enough to disorient the wolf I shoot. When the rest of the pack stops their assault and starts their return to their den, we will follow."

Christina processes what has been shared. "Who is going to follow the pack? Willie hesitates before answering.

"This is the risky part. It will take all three of us guys. That leaves you ladies here with Heath. That is the only way I see this being successful. We will be exposed out there with the pack. Once we discover their den, we will return and hopefully Monica will find something in their blood that we can use to our advantage." Silence fills the room. No one has a plan B.

How are Christina and I supposed to hold off an onslaught of those creatures?" Monica asks. The three males look at each other.

"The torches you two have used seems to work the best against them. One of you should take the door, the other the window. Once you burn a few of them, they will retreat."

"But the elephant is still in the room," Jack said. "If we are successful in finding their den, then what? Rush them with a bunch of spears and torches. We don't even know how many of them we are up against."

Willie quickly responds. "You're right. The finding of their location is only part of the equation. It is up to you Monica to find something in their blood." He pauses. "Let's rest up before they come again." Jack rejoins Monica who reaches out for a hug. The two return to the blood samples.

As Stu and Willie place the team's weapons in the center of the room, Monica leans into Jack. "I read a recent publication where a zoo in Germany has been experimenting using a sedative aerosol spray versus darts. They use the spray to temporarily put animals down and then administer an IV so they could better monitor the amount of time they could keep the animal down."

"Assuming that would work, we need to device a way to distribute the sedative and make it airborne, but how? We only have limited equipment at our disposal," Jack replied.

"Like I said, it was just a research article," she said, giving him a kiss on his forehead.

"Let me try something," he said while placing a new petri dish under his microscope.

He takes a small dose of sedative and blows it into a petri dish. After a few seconds, he turns to Monica excitedly

"Look at this."

Monica leans over and looks into his microscope. "What am I looking for?"

"Look at the activity of the blood cells with only a small dose of the sedative." She looks back and her slide and returns to Jack's microscope.

"Their movement has drastically slowed down but not completely inactive," she responds.

"Correct. That means that if we can devise a method of spraying the sedative in a confined area, on a large group of them will at least temporarily knock them out or at least make them disoriented when we can dispatch them." Monica is temporarily lost in thought.

"That would work theoretically, but only if we can devise a way to make the sedatives we have into an aerosol." Monica interjects.

# CHAPTER EIGHTEEN

Suddenly, Heath sits up in his cot screaming. "Here they come! Here they come!" Everyone takes their position. Jack, Stu and Willie are armed with their spears. Willie has the dart gun in his waistband. Monica and Christina light up their torches. They wait. The assault comes from both sides.

Growls, screams and wood splintering are heard. One of the creatures reaches through the window and Jack attempts to stab it. Monica sets its fur on fire. It screams and retreats. Christina does the same at the door. Willie fires a dart into one of the creatures who pulls his arm back. Then, as quickly as the assault started, it stops. They hear the creatures retreat.

"Okay. Jack, Stu, let's go. Board up after us ladies. We will return as soon as we can," Willie demands. He opens the door slowly and sees the end of the retreating pack and the sedated creature who is having a tough time running on all fours. When he stands, he falls to his side crashing into rotting fencing. The pack does not turn to render aid but continues on. Willie, Stu and Jack follow from a safe distance.

Willie whispers to Stu and Jack. "Let's not lose him. The way he is walking, it should be easy to follow."

"Yeah, but we also have to watch out in case some of the pack returns to check on him," Stu replies.

"I doubt that. In a normal wolf pack, if one gets injured, they are left behind to care for themselves," Jack said.

"Let's hope it applies to these creatures," Willies said as they continue to trail the sedated creature.

Daylight filters through the flora. The sounds of the retreating pack have stopped. The sedated wolf continues to struggle finding its way to the den. Willie raises his hand in a fist motioning Stu and Jack to stop. "I think we are getting close. I don't hear any noises from the retreating pack. I just hope the sedative is strong enough before the creature recovers."

"Look," Jack says, pointing at the creature. "Look. It has slowed down. It's shaking its head. The sedation must be wearing off."

"Over there," Willie said, while pointing to an area ahead of the recovering creature. "In the side of that hill. There's an opening."

Stu covers his nose. "Yeah. I see it. Do you guys smell that?"

"It's coming from over there. There is a pile of excrement like we found in the swimming pool enclosure," Willie replied.

"Guess they don't want to shit inside their den," a smiling Jack added.

"Let's hold our position here and see if the wounded animal goes inside," Willie ordered.

They watch. The sedated creature stands upright and smells the air. The three hold their breath. He finally falls to all four legs and walks into the cave.

"That's it. We found their hangout," an excited Willie claims. "Let's get out of here."

"But we don't know how many of them there are nor how big the inside of their den is," Jack said.

Willie turns and looks at Jack and Stu. "Getting any closer will bring out the pack. We can't risk that. We have to get back to the girls and prepare for their next attack." They start their retreat, just as two creatures come out of the den sniffing the air.

Willie points to a stream. "Quick, get into that stream and try to stay underwater as long as you can. That should interrupt our scent." They slowly enter the water trying not to make a splash. Willie looks back and sees the two creatures sniffing and coming their way. Willie pulls out a knife and cuts three pieces of hollow reed. He motions to Stu and Jack to use it as a breathing tube. They follow his instruction. They go under the water. Looking up they can see the two creatures sniffing the air. After a few minutes, the creatures leave.

Monica diligently guards the window while Christina watches the outside through several gaps in the wooden door. “Do you think they are okay?” a nervous Monica asks.

“I sure hope so. If the creatures act like wolves, they will hightail it back to their den and will care less about the sedated one. Assuming the drugs does not wear out too soon, they should have not trouble tailing it back to the den.”

Monica looks at Heath. “How is Heath doing?” Christina shakes her head indicating that he is not doing well.

Christina strokes his forehead. “He needs to be in a hospital. All I can do is make him as comfortable as I can. How are you doing on the blood samples?”

“Actually, Jack made a discovery. It turns out that the sedatives we have, when administered via a spray or aerosol is effective. For how long, we don’t know.”

“So, if we can find a way to spray the sedative into their den, in a confined space, we can effectively knock them out. Once unconscious, we can permanently eliminate them.”

“Theoretically, yes, Monica replies.

Christina laughs. “I hate it when you scientists say theoretically.” Monica returns the laugh. They hear movement outside. Both light their torches and wait nervously. Just then, Willie calls out.

"Christina. Monica. Open the door." Christina quickly opens the door allowing Willie, Stu and Jack enter. "You can put the torches out. They did not follow us." Monica runs to Jack and gives him a hugs Jack.

"Were you able to find out where those asshole live?" Christina asks.

"Yes. They are not here in the abandoned apartments. We followed the sedated one who followed the pack to a large cave in a hill."

"Do you know how many there are?" asked Monica.

"No. We barely got back alive," an out of breath, Jack responds.

Moncia, alarmed, looks up at Jack. "What happened?"

Before Jack could answer, Stu jumped in. "We followed the drugged creature to the cave. After he entered, two came out and began smelling the air. They looked in our direction and started for us."

Monica puts her hand over her mouth. "Oh my God. What did you do?"

"Thanks to the resourcefulness of Willie here, he told us to dive in a creek where he gave us some hollow reeds to use as a snorkel. We hid underwater until the creatures gave up and returned to their den," Jack responded.

"We owe Willie our lives," added Stu.

"Let's not get all Hallmark," a smiling Willie said. "Now that we know where they live, what is our plan?"

"Monica has some good news," an excited Christina announced. All eyes turn to Monica.

"It was actually Jack who made a breakthrough. Before you three left, he put some of the mutant wolf blood in a petri dish. He then blew some of the sedative onto the blood. The activity of the blood cells drastically slowed down, indicating that the sedative is effective as an aerosol."

Willie gives Jack a high-five. "Way to go Jack. But how in the hell do we find a way to spray the supply of sedatives we have and get it into their den?

"I have been giving that a lot of thought while you were gone," said Monica. "When we entered this apartment, I saw an emergency cabinet in front of the complex that had a fire extinguisher."

"So?" a confused Stu asks.

"The three most common types of fire extinguishers are: air pressurized water, CO2 (carbon dioxide), and dry chemical," Monica starts to explain.

"I still don't understand how a damn fire extinguisher can help up battle those things," Stu replies.

Monica turns to Stu. "Fire requires fuel, heat, and oxygen to burn. Fire extinguishers apply an agent that will cool burning heat, smother fuel or remove oxygen so the fire cannot continue to burn."

Jack continues, "Most commonly used fire extinguisher use Carbon dioxide (CO2). It is stored in extinguishers in a liquid state. It vaporizes when released thereby smothering a fire by excluding the air (oxygen) needed for combustion."

Christina grasps the idea. "As you trigger the device, a surge of CO2 is released. If we strategically introduce our sedative solutions into this CO2 rush, it'll effectively disseminate the sedative throughout the area......"

Willie excitedly finishes her sentence. "...Into the cave, knocking those bastards out. Then we can enter and finish them off.

"Theoretically," Monica says, looking at Christina with a smiling. Christina does the same.

Willie, after processing all that had been said, addresses the group. "If these creatures keep to their schedule as they have in the past, we have time to enter several of the abandoned housing units and collect as many fire extinguishers as we can. Okay. Christina, you and Monica remain here. The three of us will gather up the extinguishers. How many do we need?"

"That is where we need to come up with an additional plan," Monica answers. "Assuming we find extinguishers in working order; and by the way, you need to test them before bringing them here, we are confronted with how to enter their den undetected." No one answers as glances are exchanged.

A frustrated Willie looks out of a crack in the door and sees the spare tire still creating black smoke in the air." "Damn. I thought we were on to something."

# CHAPTER NINETEEN

Jack snaps his fingers. "What if we do this. We know with certainty that they will attack us again in a few hours, right? If we can get enough fire extinguishers and rig them up with the sedative mixture, once we hold them off and they retreat, we follow them. Once they are back in their den, we assault them with our new aerosol spray."

"I like it," Willies said. "The guys will carry the extinguishers. The girls will carry our spears which we will use to finish them off once we knock them out."

Stu shakes his head indicating he doesn't agree. "What don't you like about my plan, Stu?" Willie asks.

"I like the plan, but the creature's sense of smell and almost superhuman hearing makes it almost impossible to sneak up on them. Remember our time in the water?"

Jack agrees with Stu. "He's right. We barely got away and didn't even get close to the entrance to the cave."

"I have an idea," Christina said. "But, once you three got into the water, they lost your scent, right?"

"Yeah, but we can't swim into their cave," a dejected Willie replies.

"Of course not. But why can't we disguise our scent with theirs? Even if they hear us, they won't be able to track us since they will be smelling themselves."

"I don't follow," Jack says. Christina looks at Willie.

"When you were in the swimming pool enclosure, you found a pile of excrement from the creatures. I suggest that we coat ourselves in their excrement and use it do disguise our scent." No one says anything until Monica breaks the ice.

"Well, we all knew it was going to be a shitty job." Everyone breaks into laughter.

Willie takes command again. "Alright then. First the guys collect the fire extinguishers.

Make sure they work. We come back here and drop them off. We then head to the swimming pool enclosure and get dirty. Then we come back and wait for their next assault.

He establishes eye contact with everyone. Spears are picked up and the team, minus Christina and Monica leave in search of fire extinguishers.

The three guys cautiously walk from building complex to the next among littered debris. They pass the abandoned Ferris wheel and bumper cars and enter the first complex. Willie motions to two fire extinguishers. "Try those two.

Stu and Jack each grab one. They test them. Neither work. They walk down a hallway until they find another cabinet with two more extinguishers. Both work. They go back outside. "Lets leave these two extinguishers here. We will collect them on our way back, Willie instructs. They continue to walk down the street to the next complex. This goes on for several blocks.

"Okay. Let's take a short break," a sweaty Willie remarks. "According to my watch, we should have enough time to collect the ones that work and then get the girls and head to the swimming pool enclosure." They lean up against a wall of an abandoned unit. Willie looks around Pripyat. "This place still gives me the creeps."

"I know," Jack replies. "I know. What keeps haunting me is what Christina said when I was reading that book of how the explosion in the nuclear reactor happened. Her words, "you mean that all happened due to a test?"

Stu agrees. "Yeah. That got to me also."

"So. Jack. Are you and Monica an official couple?" Willie asks.

Jack hesitates before answering. "I want us to be but since we are both so damn career oriented, we are afraid that a committed relationship would not last between us."

Willie smiles. "Well, if the team can find a cure for cancer after we get out of here, I don't think you two will have any career roadblocks. Your biggest concern will be where to invest all of your money." Willie turns to Stu.

"What about you Stu? Any idea what you will be doing with your fame and fortune assuming we find a cure?"

"First, I would pay off my student debt. It's not as bad as Heath's, Monica's or yours Jack, but it is up there. Then I want to pay off my parent's mortgage and let them consider retirement."

"Yeah. All that is fine and good, but what will you be doing after our discovery is made known to the public? The amount of money we will be offered by major drug companies will be off the charts," Jack inquires.

"Well, this will sound stupid, but I will buy a large yacht and sail world. There are some many places I want to explore and then, once I get that out of my system, I hope to find a good wife and start a family."

"Good for you," Willie said.

"What about you, big guy? Do you have a little honey stashed away that we don't know about?" Jack asked.

"Funny you asked that. Just before we left on this little adventure, I was contacted by my high school sweetheart. She went to one of those high school reunions and met a friend of mine who told her how to reach me. She's divorced now and, well, once I get back, she and I will go out on a date. We'll see what happens after that." In the distance the howl of a wolf could be heard. "I guess that is our warning to start heading back."

Inside the apartment, Monica and Christina could hear the clanging of fire extinguishers. As the sound got closer, they opened the door and the three guys entered. They help the three place the extinguishers on the floor.

"Great job, guys," a congratulatory Monica said. "What do we have here. I count eight."

Willie answered. "I know that is too many to carry with us, but since so many did not work when we tried them, we brought back as many as we could in working order. Hopefully you can decide which are the best and hook them up to the sedative solution."

"We heard a wolf howl in the distance. Not one of the creatures, but perhaps a wakeup call to prepare for their attack," Stu added to the conversation. Christina gives each of them a sandwich and drink which they quickly eat.

"Did you see anything interesting out there?" Christina asks.

"No, but it was still a little spooky. All those empty rooms with stuff that was left behind so many years ago," Stu replies.

Willie looks at his watch. "Time to head to the swimming pool complex. Again, you two ladies, stay behind with Heath. Give us a couple of plastic bags and we will bring back some shit for the two of you."

Christina smiles. "I love you too, Willie." She hands a few plastic bags to Willie and the opens the door.

Willie looks at Stu and Jack. "Okay. Let's make this quick and simple as they say, it's a dirty job, but someone has to do it." Stu and Jack laugh. They reach the swimming pool complex and slowly enter. A wolf is seen near a side door. Willie picks up a rock and throws it at him. He turns with a snarl on his face but then exits the building. They walk over to the large pile of creature excrement.

Willie, satisfied that there are no other wolves, instructs Stu and Willie to dig in. "Let's go. We don't have much time. Fills the bags with the shit and let's get out of here."

Christina and Monica see the three returning with sacks and open the door. "Quick. Everyone cover yourself with their shit. They are coming," instructs Willie.

"What about Heath?" Christina asks, directing her question to Willie.

"We will have to leave him alone. After we fend the pack off, we will have a long time before they return. And, if we are lucky and can kill them off in their den, no rush." The four start rubbing shit onto their clothing, face, and hands.

"I think I'm going to throw up. What the hell do these guys eat?" Christina asks. Everyone turns and stares at her, causing her to realize the stupidity of her question. "Sorry. Sorry. Dumb question. When everyone finished Willie gave them a once over.

"This is the shittiest team I have ever seen," Willie says with a smile on his face. Everyone laughs. Suddenly, Heath sits up agitated. "We know what that means. Everyone take your places. Remember, after we hold them off, we start heading to their den."

The assault starts. Growling, ripping at the door, hands coming through the broken boarded up window are met with fire from torches held by Monica and Christina. The creatures are held off again.

Willie looks at the window and then back to the group. "Alright. They are in retreat. Monica and Christina will carry our spears with theirs. Each of us guys should carry two extinguishers. Try not to let them clang together."

"Monica. You did a nice job on securing the sedation solution in front of the extinguisher. The solution should disperse easily once we set off the canisters," Jack said. Willie looks at everyone. Heath is laying comfortably on his cot.

"Let's get those bastards!" Willie shouts. They file out making their way through the city of Pripyat before entering the forest. Willies turns to the group. "No need to rush. We know where we are going. I'm not worried about them picking up our scent, but with their hearing....

No one responds. They continue their way through the forest and find a large log down across the stream that Willie, Stu and Jack hid. They cross without any water getting on their clothes. Willie raises his fist indicating for the group to stop. They were near the cave.

"Everyone get settled," Willie commands. " Let's hope these assholes go to sleep early. Stu and I will take the first watch. The rest of you, try and relax. Monica rests her head on Jack's chest. They both close their eyes. Christina moves closer to Willie and Stu. She whispers to Willie and Stu.

"How are we going to assault the den?"

"I was just thinking about that. I think that Stu, Jack, and I just rush in firing off the extinguishers. You and Monica should stay outside and spear any of the creatures that try to escape. Monica told me that the C02 will also blind them and cause them to panic. That is good for us since they will start to inhale the sedative. Stu, Jack, and I will have our mouths cover with cloth that Monica gave us." Christina does not give a reply, thinking over the plan.

"Christina. You and Monica cannot freeze up. If any of these creatures try to exit the cave, you both have to impale them. You understand? You can't hesitate. One swipe of their claws and you are done for."

"I understand Willie and I will make sure Monica understands also. After a long period of time, no sounds are coming from the den. Willie nods at Stu who wakes up Jack and Monica. Christina prepares to give Stu, Willie and Jack small spears that they put in their waistband. Monica and Christina are armed. Willie turns and looks at Stu and Jack and gives final instructions.

"Make sure our masks are on. The three of us will charge straight ahead firing off our first extinguisher. Immediately fall to your knees shooting up in the air. Be prepared for chaos. The creatures will be blinded by the CO2 but so will we."

"They will thrash about so after you empty your second extinguisher, stay low to the ground to avoid their claws. Once your first extinguisher empties, stay low and fire off your second. If everything goes as plan, in a few seconds they should all be out." He takes a deep breath followed by everyone else.

"If you're religious like I am, now's the time to pray." He pauses. "Alright lets slowly approach. When I yell, as they say, unleash hell." They leave the foliage of the forest and enter the den. Snoring could be heard.

# CHAPTER TWENTY

Inside the den, a few creatures turnover in their sleep. There are over twenty of them and among them children size creatures. Willie looks at Stu and Jack before he yells. "NOW!

The three start firing off their extinguishes will falling to the ground. The large cave quickly fills with CO2 as well as the sedative. As predicted the larger creatures begin clawing at the air. Some start to fall. Other continue to struggle.

One breaks through to escape. An inhuman scream is heard at the entrance. After a few minutes that seemed liked hours, the den is quiet. Neither Willie, Stu, or Jack could see for a few minutes. The creature who escaped exits the cave shaking its head. It saw Monica and Christina. Enraged, he charged. Monica and Cristina place the base of their spear in the ground. Both spears enter the creature's body. The momentum propels him over the two ladies. Willie runs to the entrance and finds Monica and Christina standing over an impaled creature-dead.

Willie looks at the two ladies and nods. "Quick. Bring in the spears so we can finish them off."

Monica and Christina follow Willie into the cave. They are shocked to see so many creatures, especially children among them.

"Don't look at the younger ones as anything other than a small creature. If not destroyed by us, they will prey on whoever follows us." Stu and Jack follow Willie around the room impaling each of the large and small creatures. Some make sounds, others do not.

Monica and Christina just turn away and don't participate. Exhausted, Stu, Jack and Willie stand next to the ladies and look over the carnage. "That should be the lot of them," Willie says. "Let's head back to camp and check on Heath."

Bloodied, the team walks through the forest back to their apartment. You think we can stop at the creek and dive in getting this shit off of us, Monica asks. Everyone laughs.

"Actually, that sounds like a good idea," Willie said as he becomes the first to enter the stream. They make it back to the safe confines of the apartment. "Now what?" Stu asks.

"Now we wait until the cavalry arrives. They must have seen the smoke from your tire by now," Willie says while looking through the crack in the door. Let's keep the place boarded up just in case."

"You think there might be more?" Monica asks.

"Always be prepared. Anything to eat?" Willie asks. Christina tenderly places another damp cloth on Heath's forehead. Her movements gentle and comforting as she tries to alleviate his suffering.

"Stu, you Jack and Monica should start loading up your equipment. Once the Ukrainian military shows up, I want to be ready to get the hell out of here, Willie said while eating part of an apple he found among their supplies.

"Just our equipment. None of the other stuff?" Jack inquires.

"Not unless you are planning on staying once the rest of us leave," Willie answers with a smile.

"Yeah. Like that is going to happen," Jack retorts with a laugh. Everyone is busy packing. Massive growls are heard. Willie looks out of the crack in the door and is shocked by what he sees. More and more creatures are advancing.

"There are more this time!" Heath's voice echoed through the room, his words a grim reminder of the escalating danger they faced. Heath's sudden announcement jolted the group into action, their hearts pounding with adrenaline as they prepared for the imminent onslaught. Without hesitation, Christina and Monica ignited their torches, casting flickering shadows that danced across the walls as they stood poised for battle.

Willie, Jack, and Stu rushed to the windows and door, scanning the darkness for any sign of the approaching creatures, but the landscape remained eerily silent and still. As the creatures drew nearer, their hideous sounds filled the air in a cacophony of shrill cries and guttural snarls that sent shivers down the spines of those inside the safe area. Though their assailants remained hidden from view, the chorus of their vocalizations allowed the group to anticipate their coordinated attack.

"Shit!" Willie's voice rang out urgently. "There must be at least fifteen of them on this side!"

"Same over here," Stu confirmed, his grip tightening on his spear as he ensured the makeshift defenses mounted to the floor were secure. The room filled with smoke as Christina and Monica wielded their torches, their flames casting an eerie glow over the scene as they braced themselves for the impending battle.

"Here they come!" Willie's warning reverberated through the room, a signal for the group to steel themselves for the onslaught.

A transformation began to unfold within Heath amid the chaos and clamor of the battle. His features contorted with pain as his ears lengthened resembling a wolf's but far larger and more menacing. His body swelled with unnatural growth, his clothes tearing apart at the seams as his form distorted before his companions' eyes. Saliva dripped from his gnashing jaws as he called out to the creatures outside, his voice a chilling echo of their own.

The sudden revelation of Heath's transformation sent shockwaves of horror through those inside, their shouts and cries blending with the unearthly shrieks of the creatures outside. With a gut-wrenching scream, Heath launched himself into the fray, his once-familiar face twisted into a grotesque visage of primal fury.

In a moment of clarity amidst the chaos, Christina dropped her torch and raised her spear, her movements swift and decisive. With a single, precise thrust, she impaled Heath, his agonized scream piercing the air as he fell to the floor in a writhing heap. The room fell silent save for the echoes of their ragged breaths in a grim reminder of the devastating toll of the horrors they faced.

The creatures outside suddenly halted their advance, their eerie stillness giving the impression of mourning their fallen comrade. Or perhaps it was the distant rumble of approaching helicopters and the unmistakable chatter of machine gun fire that froze them in their tracks. All at once, the air was filled with chaos as the Ukrainian army unleashed their assault against the encroaching horde.

"Everyone, take cover!" Willie's screaming voice cut through the clamor in a desperate plea as the walls of their enclosure quivered under the onslaught of stray bullets. The cacophony of machine gun fire mingled with the anguished shrieks of the dying creatures, the symphony of destruction seeming to stretch on for an eternity to those huddled within the safety of their refuge.

Finally, as the smoke began to clear, the only sound that remained was the rhythmic thrum of rotor blades slicing through the air. With trembling hands, Willie and Jack cautiously approached the door, peering out through the narrow cracks to assess the aftermath of the battle.

At least two helicopters had touched down nearby, their armed occupants advancing methodically toward their location. "We need a white flag or something," Willie muttered, his mind racing for a solution amidst the chaos.

Without hesitation, Monica tore open her sweat-soaked blouse, revealing a vibrant blue bra beneath. With a determined nod, she handed the fabric to Willie, who affixed it to the end of his spear and thrust it through the crack in the door. One of the soldiers spotted the makeshift flag, signaling to his comrades to hold their fire.

He called out in Ukrainian. His words were lost on the bewildered group within. Monica's voice rang out in response, her words urgent as she declared their nationality. Finally, a Ukrainian soldier bellowed in English, his voice a beacon of hope in the darkness.

"The creatures are gone," he shouted, his words carrying the promise of salvation. "You can come outside."

The group emerged from their shelter cautiously, blinking in the harsh light of dawn as they surveyed the battle's aftermath. The air was heavy, reeking of smoke and blood as haunting reminders of the horrors they had faced. Christina paused for a moment longer, her gaze lingering on Heath's twisted form, now transformed into one of the grotesque creatures they had fought so desperately against. Tears welled in her eyes as she silently paid her respects in a gentle acknowledgment of the friend they had lost to the horrors of the night.

Outside, the street lay strewn with the bodies of the fallen creatures, their twisted forms a grim testament to the violence that had unfolded. A group of soldiers moved swiftly among them, dispatching any that showed signs of life with ruthless efficiency. The echoes of gunfire filled the air as they worked, the sharp crack of bullets mingling with the anguished cries of the dying creatures.

A second team followed in their wake, dousing the corpses with gasoline before setting them ablaze. The acrid scent of smoke filled the air as flames consumed the remains, casting flickering shadows across the desolate landscape. It was a grim task but necessary to ensure the threat posed by the creatures was extinguished once and for all.

As the flames licked hungrily at the twisted forms of their fallen foes, the survivors stood together in solemn silence, their hearts heavy with the weight of loss and the knowledge of all they had endured. However, amid the ashes of destruction, there was also a glimmer of hope—a chance for a new beginning, free from the shadow of fear that had plagued them for so long.

# CHAPTER TWENTY-ONE

The hospital waiting room hummed with quiet tension as Willie, Jack, Stu, and Monica occupied their respective seats. Each wore an expression of mixed emotions—anticipation, anxiety, and a lingering sense of relief that they had made it this far.

"I hate this waiting," Willie said. "I need a candy bar." He walked off from the group in search of a vending machine.

"So, any guesses on the baby's gender?" Stu ventured, his attempt at levity punctuating the solemn atmosphere. "Since Christina opted not to have a scan to reveal the sex of the infant."

Jack offered a hesitant smile. "I'm betting on a girl. What about you, Monica?"

Monica shrugged, her gaze drifting off as if lost in thought. "I have a feeling it might be a boy, but who knows?"

Jack nodded, his fingers fidgeting nervously in his lap. "I just hope Christina and the baby are both healthy. She's been through a lot with Heath and…" he failed to complete his thought.

As they whiled away the time with idle chatter, the minutes stretched into hours, each passing moment bringing them closer to the momentous event they had gathered for. Despite their efforts to distract themselves, the suspense of the arrival of Christina and Heath's baby hung heavy, added to the silent reminder of the journey they had all endured together.

Finally, a hushed murmur rippled through the waiting room as a nurse emerged from the delivery room, her expression inscrutable. With a solemn nod, she announced, "Your friend's baby is on its way."

Rising to their feet, the group exchanged anxious glances as they watched the nurse re-enter the delivery room. The air was charged with anticipation as they waited with bated breath for the news they had been anxiously awaiting.

"Alright, Christina. You are now fully dilated. A few good pushes and we can welcome your baby into the world," the doctor announced, his voice strained with a forced cheerfulness that did little to mask the underlying tension in the room.

"Okay, push," the doctor instructed.

With a deep breath, Christina's body tensed with effort as she followed the doctor's instructions. "I see its head. Already looks like a full head of hair. How about another push? Ready, one, two, three, push."

As the baby made its entrance into the world, the room fell silent, the only sound the ragged gasps of the exhausted mother. But then, as the doctor's hands reached out to receive the newborn, a gasp of horror echoed through the room.

The doctor's initial shock was tangible, his hands freezing in midair as he stared down at the tiny, writhing form before him. A look of sheer disbelief crossed the face of one of the nurses, her eyes widening in terror before she quickly turned away, unable to bear the sight before her.

Christina, her body trembling with exhaustion and fear, held her breath, her heart pounding in her chest as she waited for the news she had been longing for. "The baby… it's…" the doctor began, his voice trailing off into a stunned silence.

Before he could utter another word, the infant emitted a ghastly sound—a sound that sent shivers down the spines of all present in the room. It was a sound unlike anything they had ever heard before, a chilling wail that seemed to reverberate through the very walls of the hospital.

Caught in the grip of sheer terror, Christina squeezed her eyes shut, a wave of dread washing over her as she realized that her deepest nightmare had come true. In that moment, the boundaries between reality and horror blurred, leaving them all to confront the unthinkable truth that lay before them.

# CHERNOBYL TODAY

Chernobyl, a city situated within the Chernobyl exclusion zone in the Vyshhorod Raion (district) of northern Kyiv Oblast, Ukraine, stands as a haunting testament to one of the most devastating nuclear disasters in history. Approximately 90 kilometers north of Kyiv and 160 kilometers southwest of Gomel, Belarus, Chernobyl was once home to around 14,000 residents, significantly fewer than neighboring Pripyat.

Despite being predominantly deserted today, a few brave souls still inhabit Chernobyl, dwelling in houses marked with signs asserting ownership. A small population of animals also roams its abandoned streets, and workers tasked with overseeing the Chernobyl exclusion zone find residence there. The city boasts two general stores and a hotel, albeit amid an eerie silence that belies its tumultuous past.

Construction of the Chernobyl Nuclear Power Plant, officially known as the Vladimir Ilyich Lenin Nuclear Power Plant commenced on August 15, 1972, approximately 15 kilometers northwest of Chernobyl. The plant was erected alongside Pripyat, a purpose-built 'atomograd' city founded on February 4, 1970, to support the burgeoning nuclear industry. The decision to establish the power plant in this location was made by the Central Committee of the Communist Party of the Soviet Union and the Council of Ministers of the Soviet Union, following recommendations from the State Planning Committee of the Ukrainian SSR. It marked Ukraine's inaugural venture into nuclear energy production.

However, Chernobyl's recent history has been marred by more than just nuclear energy ambitions. During the 2022 Russian invasion of Ukraine, the city fell under temporary occupation by Russian forces between February 24 and April 2. This occupation resulted in a brief surge in radiation levels attributed to various human activities, including earthworks that disturbed radioactive dust.

Access to Chernobyl and its surrounding exclusion zone is heavily regulated, primarily due to safety and security concerns. Unauthorized entry is strictly prohibited, with visitors required to enlist the services of authorized tour operators. The exclusion zone boundary, though minimally fenced and patrolled, is subject to stringent monitoring, especially around vehicular checkpoints.

Pripyat is more extensively guarded and fenced off, owing to its status as an 'attractive nuisance,' rife with hazards like structurally unsound buildings, radioactive contamination, and criminal activity. Squatting within Pripyat's confines is strongly discouraged, with regulated tour operators present daily to oversee activities and deter unauthorized access.

Those venturing into the exclusion zone must adhere to specific regulations, including obtaining a day pass from accredited tour operators at least ten days in advance. The severity of consequences for non-compliance varies, ranging from expulsion to permanent deportation from Ukraine, with foreigners facing stringent repercussions.

Given the dynamic nature of radiation levels within the exclusion zone, visitors are advised against independent exploration without professional guidance and monitoring equipment. The risk of contamination is ever-present, with exposure to higher radiation levels potentially leading to long-term health implications.

Navigating the abandoned structures within the exclusion zone poses additional dangers, with broken glass, unstable flooring, and debris littering the premises. Protective clothing, closed-toe footwear, and thorough decontamination procedures are essential to minimize the risk of radiation exposure and contamination.

Ultimately, while Chernobyl's tragic legacy continues to cast a shadow over its desolate landscape, stringent regulations and precautions remain paramount to ensuring the safety of those who dare to tread within its radioactive embrace.

# PHOTOS OF CHERNOBYL

## BEFORE THE EXPLOSION

МИРУ МИР
СЛАВА КПСС
ЭНЕРГЕТИКИ ЧЕРНОБЫЛЬСКОЙ АЭС ИМ. В. И. ЛЕНИНА ОБЯЗА СЬ ПЛАН
РЕАЛИЗАЦИИ ПРОДУКЦИИ ВЫПОЛНИТЬ К 22 ДЕКАБР 1983 ГОДА

May Day Parade the day before the explosion.

# AFTER THE EXPLOSION

ПРИПЯТЬ
1970

4
3

# OTHER HORROR NOVELS BY THE AUTHOR:

## HOUSE ON HAUNTED HILL RESURRECTION

*House on Haunted Hill: Resurrection* is a contemporary reimagining of the iconic Vincent Price horror film. After serving a twenty-year sentence for his wife's murder in the notorious House on Haunted Hill, Frederick Loren decides to host another haunted house party with a sinister agenda: to expose several self-proclaimed psychics as frauds.

Seven individuals, each harboring their own flaws, eagerly accept Loren's invitation, enticed by the promise of a $100,000 prize if they survive the night. Unbeknownst to the guests, the mansion's previous owner, Watson Pritchard, firmly believes in its haunted nature, and his convictions prove chillingly accurate. The malevolent spirit of Inquisitor Torquemada, along with his bloodthirsty henchmen, awakens from its slumber after years of dormancy, fixating its supernatural wrath on the unsuspecting guests.

## THE TINGLER UNLEASHED

*The Tingler Unleashed* is a contemporary reimagining that pays homage to the 1959 cinematic masterpiece by William Castle, featuring the incomparable Vincent Price. The film's narrative revolves around a brilliant scientist unraveling the existence of a peculiar parasite dwelling within humans, christened the 'tingler.' This minuscule entity thrives on fear, inducing a spine-tingling sensation in its host whenever terror strikes.

Dr. Warren Chapin, a dedicated pathologist, unearths the truth behind the spine-tingling phenomenon, attributing it to the growth of a peculiar creature residing within every human—an aptly named 'tingler.'

## CARNIVAL OF LOST SOULS

Step into the eerie world of *Carnival of Lost Souls*, a contemporary reimagining of the 1962 American psychological horror film *Carnival of Souls*. In a chilling twist of fate, our female protagonist survives a harrowing car only to find herself teetering on the precipice of sanity. Haunting hallucinations beckon her to a long-forgotten, desolate carnival ground, where an insidious serial killer lurks in the shadows, determined to snuff out her life. Sixty-one years later, the tale is reborn with a fresh layer of suspense and intrigue.

## BENEATH THE EARTH

Set in the desolate landscape of Russia, a group of American scientists find themselves plunged into a nightmarish battle for survival when they venture into the depths of the abandoned Kola Superdeep Borehole.

When seismic activity causes the long-forgotten borehole to erupt, it releases a malevolent force into the world – gigantic acid-spewing spiders that have lurked beneath the Earth's surface for centuries. As the creatures emerge from the depths, the Russian government urgently requests the expertise of American scientists to assess the situation and contain the growing threat.

## SEAL: GHOST RECON

In the chilling reimagining of a classic Night Gallery episode, *SEAL – Ghost Recon* takes readers on a heart-pounding journey into the depths of fear and bravery.

Meet Ryan 'Falcon' Foster, a Navy SEAL sniper with a reputation for boasting about his courage that is, as yet, untested in the face of true terror.

When a dare challenges Falcon to spend a night inside a notorious haunted house for a chance at a hefty $25,000 prize, he cannot resist. Armed to the teeth and fueled by bravado, he steps into the eerie mansion, oblivious to the spectral entities that await him in the shadows.

# JEANNIE LOOMIS THRILLER NOVELS:

*Ark of the Covenant - Raid on the Church of Our Lady Mary of Zion*

*Star Chamber*

*Forgotten Plans*

*House of Special Purpose*

*Time Game*

*Thin Blue Line*

*The Fourth Reich*

*Black Heart/Black Cell*

*The Phantom Train*

*Rollercoaster*

*Snow Angel*

*The Fourth Reich Reborn*

*Relics of Redemption*

www.ingramcontent.com/pod-product-compliance
Lightning Source LLC
Chambersburg PA
CBHW020557310726
48979CB00008B/1253/J

* 9 7 9 8 9 8 9 3 4 2 4 8 8 *